Looking

For

Lainey

by

KRISTEN MIDDLETON

To my readers...

May your children always be safe

and sound.

Other books by author Kristen Middleton

Blur
Shiver
Vengeance
Illusions

Venom
Slade
Toxic
Claimed by the Lycan

Jezebel
Deviant

Enchanted Secrets
Enchanted Objects
Enchanted Spells

Origins
Running Wild
Dead Endz
Road Kill
End Zone

Paxton VS The Undead

Planet Z
Blood of Brekkon

Romance under pen name K.L. Middleton

Recommended For ages 18 and older due to sexual situations and language.

Tangled Beauty
Tangled Mess
Tangled Fury

Sharp Edges

Billionaire at Sea
Billionaire at Sea Book 2

Gritty biker romance under pen name Cassie Alexandra

For ages 18 and older. Vulgar language and sexual content.

Resisting the Biker
Surviving the Biker
Fearing the Biker
Breaking the Biker
Taming the Biker
Loving the Biker

Chapter 1

Lainey

Friday, November 24th

8:45 p.m.

"CAN I LOOK at the Barbie dolls?" eight-year-old Lainey Brown asked her mother.

Beth, who was searching through endless rows of Legos for a gift for her boyfriend's son, pushed the cart slowly down the aisle. "Not tonight. We're looking for a present for Mason and I'm pretty sure he doesn't want one of those," she replied, smiling. "Why don't you help me pick something out for him? Mike said he loves Legos. I just don't know which one to choose."

"I don't know what he likes," answered Lainey sullenly. "And I don't want to go to his stupid birthday party."

Her words surprised Beth. It didn't sound like Lainey at all. Of course, she was probably tired. Normally, her daughter was in bed by nine. "That's not very nice."

"*He's* not nice. He pulled my hair last night, and then called me a baby when I told him that it hurt. But… it did hurt. A lot." She pouted.

Beth had to admit that Mason, who was turning eleven in two days, *was* a little shit. But, he was also Mike's son and the two children needed to learn to get along.

"I'm sorry he hurt you. Just ignore him when he gets like that."

7

"I tried to, and that's when he pulled my hair."

Beth glanced at Lainey's long, shiny, blonde hair. She didn't like the idea of Mason, or anyone else, pulling at it either. "If he does something like that again, let me or Mike know."

Her forehead scrunched up. "But you said I shouldn't be a tattletale."

"This is different. When someone is hurting you, I want you to come forward and say something."

"Okay." Lainey sighed. "Are we going home soon?"

"Yes. After I find something."

Lainey pointed. "The Barbie aisle is just on the other side. Can I go and look at them?"

Maybe I should give Mason a Barbie, Beth mused to herself, since he's so obsessed with blonde hair. "Fine. But, remember, we're buying a gift for someone else."

"I know," said Lainey, already rushing away.

LAINEY TURNED AROUND the corner and began searching for the doll she'd seen on television. The one with the hair you could grow, color, and style any way you wanted. It didn't take her long to locate it. Reaching up, she grabbed the Barbie and stared at it, wishing it was going home with her. A girl at school, Kylee, said she'd gotten it recently and Lainey wanted one so badly herself. She dreamed about all the different ways she could change the doll's hair color, and wished her mother would buy it.

I have to ask her.

Taking a deep breath, she walked back over to the Lego aisle. "Mom, can we please, *please* get this?" Lainey begged, hoping her mother would give in, like she sometimes did.

Beth looked at the package she held and groaned. "I told you, we can't. Christmas is coming soon. Maybe you'll get one then."

She stared at the doll longingly. "But, what if they run out?"

"I doubt they will. You have to wait, Lainey."

Pursing her lips, Lainey stomped back to the Barbie aisle. As she was about to put the doll back onto the shelf, she noticed a familiar face walking toward her. She almost didn't recognize him because of the way he was dressed. Normally, he wore nicer clothing; tonight he looked more like her gym teacher, Mr. Grayson, with the sweats and a hoodie he was wearing. He also had on a pair of eyeglasses and a baseball cap. It was a little weird.

Surprised to see him in the store, Lainey smiled and was about to ask what he was doing there, when he put his finger against his lips.

Confused, she watched as he pulled a white handkerchief out of his pocket and moved in very close to her. "Oh, look at that. You have something on your nose," he whispered, lowering it to her face. "Hold still."

The last thing Lainey remembered before blacking out was that the handkerchief was damp and smelled yucky.

BETH WAS GETTING frustrated.

Although there were plenty of Legos to choose from, most of the sets were well out of her price-range. She was a single mom on a tight budget, and used to being frugal with her money. But, she wanted to buy something Mason would like, and Legos were the one thing she was certain he'd enjoy. Plus, it would give him something to do, other than pick on Lainey.

"When did these things get so expensive?" she mumbled under her breath.

Not that she'd purchased many in the past. Lainey was her only child and had never really gotten into building blocks.

After a couple more minutes of searching, Beth settled on a set

9

that was thirty dollars higher than what she'd planned on spending, and tossed it into the cart. It was nine o'clock and almost past Lainey's bedtime. Time to go home.

"Lainey!" she called loudly. "Let's get going."

There was no answer from the other aisle.

Sighing, Beth pushed the cart around the corner and noticed she wasn't there. Beth tried the next aisle, and then the next. Unfortunately, there was no sign of her daughter.

"Lainey?" she called out, more irritated than anything. This had happened before. Lainey had a tendency to go wandering off, although usually not too far.

Beth turned the cart around and went through every one of the toy aisles, wondering if Lainey was irritating her on purpose because she was still angry about the doll. It really wasn't like her to play games, but she was developing a temper and had obviously been grumpy to begin with.

"Excuse me," Beth said to an employee walking by with a mop. "Have you seen a little girl wandering around? She's eight, has long, blonde hair, and wearing a light-blue jacket."

The woman frowned. "No. How long has she been missing for?"

"Just a few minutes," replied Beth, the word 'missing' making her stomach churn.

"Let me call in a *Code Adam*," said the woman, rushing away.

"Lainey!" Beth cried, abandoning her cart. The words "Code Adam" echoed through her head.

Where was she?

In panic-mode, she rushed past the video games and headed toward the camping gear. "Lainey!"

No answer.

Beth turned around and raced the other way, calling frantically for her daughter.

10

Over the loudspeaker, an employee announced a "Code Adam", and that's when her hysteria really began to set in.

Chapter 2

Hawk

TAKING HER IN the store had been a risky move, but it was also brilliant as far as Hawk was concerned. Nobody would suspect him of kidnapping Lainey, and he'd been especially careful with his disguise. In the end, they'd think he was some random pervert. Instead, he was a guy about to make a shitload of money.

"Oh, look at the poor dearie," said an older employee, collecting carts. The woman smiled warmly. "She must be plum tuckered out."

Hawk didn't look directly at the woman and kept his head down to avoid the cameras. The last thing he needed was to get into a conversation with some nosy, old broad. "Yes. Busy day," he replied, patting Lainey's back affectionately.

"Oh, to be that young again," the woman said with a wistful smile. "And exhausted from playing too hard."

"No doubt," he replied. "Have a good night."

"Thank you. You, too."

Still holding Lainey, he stepped outside into the darkness. Seconds later, a black Tahoe screeched to a halt next to them. The passenger jumped out and opened the back door.

Hawk quickly put Lainey inside and slid in back with her.

12

"Let's move," he said, noticing a Walmart employee approaching the front door.

The passenger slammed the door and jumped back in front. One minute later, they were on HWY 36 and heading north.

Chapter 3

Beth

LAINEY WAS NOWHERE to be found, and by the time the police showed up at the store, Beth was a total wreck.

"Ma'am, do you have any recent pictures of your daughter?" Detective Jason Samuels asked in his gravelly voice after taking her statement. He had wavy brown hair, bright blue eyes, and a hawk-like nose. Beth thought he looked a little like a young Mel Gibson.

"Yes, I have quite a few in my phone," she answered, her hands shaking as she pulled out it out of her purse. "I can send them to you."

"Okay." He gave her his number.

Beth sent him two recent pictures, her chest tightening as she looked at them. Lainey was everything to her and the thought of someone hurting her baby was too horrifying to imagine.

"I'll get her photos out. A nationwide Amber Alert has already been issued," Samuels said, scrolling through his phone and pushing buttons.

At the mention of an Amber Alert, Beth lost it. This was serious. It was real. It was frightening. Her daughter wasn't just lost. She was missing. "I can't believe this has happened," she cried, her eyes blinded by tears. "And I was right there. Right *there*!"

14

"You were in the aisle next to her. Nobody could have imagined that someone would be bold enough to… to do something like this."

He meant 'kidnap', she thought miserably. *Someone has my sweet little girl.*

"Hopefully, we'll find your daughter quickly and this will all be over," said Samuels in a gentler voice. "Have you contacted Lainey's father?"

"Yes," she replied, grabbing some tissues from the box on the table. They were in the Walmart employee breakroom located in the back of the warehouse. "Tom is on his way."

The detective nodded and went back to his phone.

The door swung open and the store manager, Don Timberland, hurried inside. "Detective, we have the video feed ready from the surveillance cameras."

"Thanks," said Samuels, shoving his phone inside his jacket. He looked at Beth. "Ready?"

She nodded.

The three walked through the store to the manager's office, where they met up with Samuel's partner, Detective Anna Dubov. Dubov was in her thirties, had short, dark hair, and kind brown eyes.

"Have *you* heard anything yet?" Dubov asked Samuels as the manager sat back down at his desk.

"No. Hopefully, the footage will help shed some light on what happened," he replied as they gathered around the manager's desk.

"It does," said the manager. "It looks like someone grabbed her while you weren't paying attention."

Samuels gave him a stern look.

"Oh, sorry," Don replied, embarrassed.

"Is… that him?" said Beth hoarsely when she saw the stranger approaching her daughter on the video. He appeared to be a

15

medium-built man, wearing a dark, hooded sweatshirt, a baseball cap, and eyeglasses.

"Looks like it," said Samuels, staring hard at the video. "Notice how he kept his head down and avoided the cameras? Almost like he knew exactly where they were located."

"He may be an employee," Dubov said.

"No. None of my employees would do something like this," Don said, frowning.

Dubov looked at him. "Disgruntled ex-employee?"

He shrugged. "Maybe."

"The man is dressed like the Unabomber," Beth said, hating the scumbag who'd taken her child. Rage and terror flooded through every fiber of her being as she watched the scene continue to unfold. When the kidnapper covered Lainey's mouth with a rag and she passed out, Beth let out a moan of despair. "Oh, my poor baby."

"That's how he managed to take her so quietly," Dubov said sadly.

Beth's eyes stared in horror as the man picked up her daughter and carried her away. Like a father might take his sleeping daughter. Turning, she gripped Samuels' arm. "You *have* to find her. Please, Detective," she choked. "Save her."

"We'll do everything we can," he replied in a solemn voice. "I promise."

"I can't believe this is happening," Beth said, feeling as if the walls were about to close in on her. She let go of his arm. "What kind of an evil monster would take a little girl like that?"

"A sick piece of shit," said Dubov, scowling at the computer.

"Here's more footage," said the manager, clicking on another image. It showed the kidnapper interacting with an employee right before walking out the front door.

"That's Gloria," said the manager. "I spoke to her. She claimed

16

she didn't get a good look at him."

"He kept his face down. Again," said Samuels, disappointed. "But, there might be something she remembers. We'll have Gloria talk to a sketch artist."

"Was there anyone else who saw him?" Beth asked, wishing Mike was there. He was in Colorado, at some kind of art convention. He, and his brother Mitch owned an art gallery in Minneapolis.

"We're still questioning everyone in the store," said Samuels. "What about the outdoor cameras? Did any of them catch anything?"

"Yeah. There's something there. The kidnapper definitely had help," said Mr. Timberland, clicking on another image.

The group watched as a newer-looking Tahoe stopped abruptly in front of the kidnapper. A tall, broad-shouldered man wearing dark clothing and a baseball cap jumped out and helped get Lainey into the vehicle.

"Is there another angle?" Samuels asked.

"Yeah," said the manager, pulling up two more videos.

Unfortunately, they didn't learn anything more about the SUV or who was inside. The license plate had been removed and the camera didn't pick up enough of the driver to get a good description.

"They've done this before," said Samuels, looking over at Dubov. "It looks too organized."

His partner nodded, a troubled look on her face.

Beth felt like there was something else they weren't saying, and it made her worry even more.

"What do they want with her? I have no money. If they're looking for a ransom, they've definitely taken the wrong kid," she said, her eyes moving from one detective to the other.

"Could be selling her," suggested Mr. Timberland, leaning back

17

in his beat-up, old, brown leather chair. He clasped his fingers together over his pot-belly. "I don't know about you, but I saw this special on the History Channel about sex-trafficking. There's a lot of it going on, even here in the United States. And parents aren't watching their kids close enough, which makes it even easier for them. If I was a father, I'd never take my eyes off of mine. No offense, Mrs. Brown."

The two detectives scowled at him.

Beth gasped and raised her hand to her mouth. "Do you think someone is selling Lainey?" She looked at Samuels. "Is it possible?"

He placed a hand on her shoulder. "Of course, we're not going to rule anything out. The truth is, we don't know for sure what's going on." He gave the manager a hard look. "And we definitely shouldn't jump to conclusions."

Mr. Timberland shrugged and returned his attention back to the computer.

"What about Lainey's father?" asked Dubov. "Would he have taken her?"

"No. Of course not," Beth replied. "Tom is a good man and can see Lainey whenever he wants. He wouldn't need to kidnap her."

"Would someone abduct her to get back at him, somehow?" she asked, sitting down on the edge of the manager's desk.

Beth sighed "I can't imagine who would. Tom doesn't have any money either. Or enemies. At least, not that I'm aware of."

"What does he do for a living?" Samuels asked.

"He's a mechanic," she replied. "He works over at Donelly's Auto Body in St. Paul."

"I know where that is. So, you two are separated?" Samuels asked, jotting more things down in his notepad.

"Divorced. Two years ago," she replied.

"What's your relationship like now?" he asked her.

18

"It's fine. I mean, we get into arguments sometimes about raising Lainey. It's nothing major, though. He's a good guy. He loves Lainey as much as I do."

"Do you have full custody?" Samuels asked.

"It's joint," replied Beth.

Samuels was silent for a few seconds, still busy writing things down. When he was finished, he glanced over at the manager. "Mr. Timberland, can you give us a few minutes alone with Mrs. Brown?"

The man stood up. "Of course. I should probably make my rounds anyway. Take all the time you need."

"Thank you," said Samuels.

He nodded and stepped out of the office, closing the door behind him.

"Is there anything we should know about your ex-husband, Mrs. Brown?" Samuels asked.

"I don't understand what you mean," Beth replied, looking puzzled.

"Pardon my asking, but… if he's such a good guy, why did you two divorce?" he asked.

She dabbed at her face with a tissue. "I don't see how the reason for our divorce is relevant to Lainey's disappearance."

"At this point, everything is relevant. She's missing and we don't want to leave any stones unturned," said Dubov softly.

Beth sighed. "We split because we argued about money all the time and it just became too stressful for everyone. As far as I was concerned, he was spending it way too foolishly. Tom didn't seem to agree."

"What do you mean?" he asked. "What was he spending it on?"

"Rebuilding this GTO he has. Every spare penny went to that damn car, and it wasn't like we could afford it. Then there was the

19

gambling," she muttered.

The two detectives both perked up.

"Really? What kind of gambling?" Samuels asked, clicking his pen again.

"Mostly poker. He has this big dream of someday becoming a professional card player. When we were together, it seemed like every Saturday night he'd drive to Treasure Island with his buddies. Sometimes he'd win, but more times than not, he'd lose. I just couldn't take it anymore. I mean, the car was one thing… he was sinking money into it, but at least it was sellable, you know?"

Samuels nodded. "So, would you say that your ex has a gambling problem?"

The office door opened up and a tall, dark-haired man walked inside, his expression stony. "Excuse me, but why aren't you people out looking for my daughter instead of talking trash about me?" he asked angrily.

Chapter 4

Saturday

1:30 a.m.

Beth

WHEN THE POLICE were finished questioning Tom, he offered Beth a ride home and she accepted. Still in shock after everything that had happened, Beth knew she wasn't in any shape to drive. Plus, the very idea that she was leaving the store without Lainey was harrowing.

"There are reporters outside," Samuels said, as they headed out of the office. "We'll accompany you to your vehicle so they don't harass you too much. Do us a favor, though, don't say anything to the press. Not now, anyway. You can give the media a statement later in the day. We'll help you with that, too."

"Okay," said Tom, looking relieved. "I noticed the crowd already gathered when I arrived. How did they find out about it so soon?"

"The Amber Alert," explained Samuels.

"Ah. Makes sense. By the way, what can *we* do, besides wait around, to help locate Lainey?" Tom asked.

"Start spreading the word that she's missing. The more people searching for her, the better," said Samuels. "And, if you remember anything else leading up to the time she was taken, Mrs. Brown, call us. Such as someone following you or paying a little too much

21

attention to Lainey."

Beth nodded. "I will. Just, please, find our daughter."

"We'll do our very best," Samuels replied. "I promise you."

The couple thanked him.

"Do you think someone will call and demand money from us?" asked Tom. "Like a ransom?"

"It's possible, but, like you mentioned earlier, neither of you are very well off," he replied. "Usually, ransom-motivated kidnappers will target someone they believe has a lot of money."

They'd questioned Tom about his finances and asked if he had any gambling debts. Tom had denied owing anything and had told the police that he'd quit going to the casinos six months before.

"But, what if someone does call about a ransom?" Beth asked.

Dubov handed Beth her card. "Keep a notepad nearby. Write down everything they tell you, and then immediately call us."

TOM AND BETH rode in silence, both of them shaken by everything that had happened.

Pulling up to her house, Tom parked in the driveway and turned off the engine. "Hopefully, the police will find her soon," he said in a weary voice.

Beth cleared her throat. "Yes."

Tom looked at the small, ranch-style house they'd once shared and sighed. "Where's Mike?"

The two men tolerated each other, although Beth knew he was jealous of Mike. Deep down, she also knew Tom still loved her, and the truth was, she still had some feelings for him. But Beth felt like she'd always taken second place to his gambling habits, even when he'd denied it.

"In Denver, at an art convention," she replied, staring ahead into the darkness, her mind still on Lainey.

22

The idea that their daughter had been kidnapped, that she was missing, felt like a knife to the heart. Beth could only imagine how terrified her little girl was and it ate her up inside, knowing she was responsible and couldn't do anything about it. She longed to hold Lainey in her arms. To soothe and protect her. To keep her safe from the monsters who had taken her. But she couldn't, and it tore at her insides.

"When is he coming back?"

"As soon as possible. He's checking for flights," she said, watching as a gust of wind blew several leaves across the windshield.

"What did he say?"

"Mike was upset, too, when he heard the news."

She thought about the conversation she'd had with him. Mike had been shocked. He'd grown to love Lainey and was good to her. Lainey, on the other hand, liked him, but still had the crazy notion that her parents would one day get back together. When she'd learned about their engagement, she'd thrown a fit.

"But Daddy still loves you," she'd cried.

"And I will always love him. But, sometimes people are happier when they're not together," Beth had told her.

As much as she'd tried to explain, Lainey still hadn't understood, which had been frustrating. But she was young, and Beth knew her daughter would learn to accept that her parents weren't going to get back together.

"What about your father?"

Beth's dad, William, was at his vacation home in Florida with Helen, her stepmother. When she'd given them the news, they'd been horrified, promising to fly back to Minnesota as soon as possible. Her father, who'd been in the military and not one to ever get too emotional, had been so distraught that he'd broken down on the phone. Lainey was his only grandchild and he adored her.

23

"They're supposed to be here later this evening. I hope," she replied, praying that by then, Lainey would already be found and safely back at home.

"Good."

She glanced at him. Her father and Tom didn't always see eye-to-eye. In fact, William had been disgusted by his son-in-law's gambling habit, especially since it had been the catalyst that led to their divorce.

"Would you mind if I stayed the rest of the night? On the couch?" he replied, rubbing his temples. "I want to be around if the police call with any updates."

Beth was relieved. Although she wanted nothing more than to curl up in Lainey's bed, the thought of being alone was depressing. "Of course."

Tom's eyes filled with fresh tears as he stared at the swing set behind the house. The one he'd built. "I just can't believe this is happening. I feel so damn... helpless," he said, his voice breaking.

"I'm so sorry, Tom," she said. She felt so guilty. Like she'd failed as a parent and it was eating her up inside. If only she'd have kept Lainey in her sight. "I shouldn't have let her wander the store alone. This is my fault."

He let out a heavy sigh. "It's not."

"I let her go. Alone."

"It's not like she was on the other side of the store. She was in the next aisle. I've gone shopping with her, Beth. I know how antsy she gets," he said.

His words didn't comfort her. She'd failed to protect their daughter, on *her* watch, and could only blame herself.

I'm a shitty mother, she thought, feeling miserable.

And one who couldn't afford to feel sorry for herself.

Beth took a deep breath. It was time to focus on what she could do now, instead of what she'd failed to do earlier.

24

"Let's go inside," Beth said, grabbing her purse. "My cell phone is about to die. I need to charge it and get on social media. Just like Detective Samuels said, we need to spread the word that our daughter is missing."

"Good idea."

TOM QUIETLY FOLLOWED Beth into the house. They went into the kitchen and he asked if he could brew a cup of coffee with the Keurig. "After all, it's not like I'm going to be able to sleep anyway."

"Go ahead."

He stared at her face. There were bags under her eyes. Something he'd never seen before. "You look exhausted. Why don't you try and rest while I sit up and wait for news? If I hear anything, I'll wake you."

"Thanks, but I'm going to post about Lainey missing on Facebook and Twitter. I doubt I'll be sleeping anytime soon," said Beth, plugging her phone into the charger. "In fact, could you make a cup for me, too? Everything is still where it was when you lived here."

He nodded and then set about making them both coffee. Once he was finished, Tom brought the cups over to the small, round oak table where Beth now sat. She had her laptop open and was logging into her Facebook account.

"Thanks," she murmured when he set a steaming cup down in front of her.

"You're welcome."

Tom sat down across from her and peered around the kitchen. It was quiet, and despite what they were going through, comforting to be there. Although he'd been by to pick up Lainey a number of times, Mike was usually around and it was awkward. Now that it was just the two of them alone, he was reminded of the many times they'd shared dinner together at the table. The conversations they'd had, both good and bad. The memories, including the time she'd surprised him with the news of being pregnant with Lainey. He would never forget that day... how she'd made his favorite carrot cake and had frosted a date on the top in bright orange.

"What is that for?" he'd asked, not understanding.

"That's the day our life is going to change forever," she'd replied, her bright blue eyes shiny with joyful tears. "It's when we're both going to be parents."

Knowing how much having a child meant to her, he'd smiled, picked her up, and twirled her around, both of them soon laughing and crying together. Although the prospect of being a father had been a little unnerving, especially back then, in the end he found that Lainey had been the best thing to ever happen to him.

Besides Beth.

And Tom had blown it. All because he'd been a selfish, stubborn asshole. The truth was, it wasn't even the gambling that had ruined their relationship. It had been the arrogant notion that *nobody* told Tom Brown what to do, including Beth. Now, he'd do anything to go back in time and fix what he'd broken.

Tom's eyes filled with tears again as he realized that *he* was actually responsible for Lainey's abduction. He'd driven the family apart and she'd found a way to heal, through Mike. If she'd never gotten into a relationship with him, Beth wouldn't have been out shopping for a gift for his son, Mason. Lainey's abduction wouldn't have ever occurred.

Seeing Tom's tears, Beth reached over and grabbed his hand.

"I don't know what to do," he said, trying not to cry. "I feel so helpless."

"I know. Just... stay strong," she said, squeezing his hand. "For Lainey. We both have to. We'll get her back, Tom. We have

26

to believe it."

Sitting there now with Beth, he was reminded of how much he'd already lost and vowed that whatever it took, he'd get them *both* back.

Chapter 5

Saturday

11:25 a.m.

Lainey

SEVERAL HOURS LATER, Lainey woke up in a dark bedroom with a pounding headache and a bad taste in her mouth.

"Mommy?" she whispered, blinking several times.

As her eyes adjusted to the darkness, Lainey began to remember what had happened and it confused and frightened her. Even worse, she was in a scary place that she didn't recognize.

With her heart pounding in her chest, Lainey got out of the bed and crept over to the door. She tried opening it, but found that the door was locked.

"Mommy!" she called, rattling the knob.

A woman began yelling angrily from somewhere in the house, speaking in a language she didn't recognize.

Scared, Lainey scampered back to the bed and crawled under the covers.

A short time later, the door opened up and the bedroom light was switched on. Lainey peeked out from under the covers and noticed a woman in a short, white robe enter the room carrying a tray of food. She thought the woman was pretty, although her lipstick was too bright and she had curlers in her red hair.

Lainey watched as the stranger approached the bed and set the tray down next to her, on the nightstand.

"Where's my mom?" she squeaked, staring up at her and trembling. It was then that Lainey noticed the woman had a long scar that ran under the side of her chin.

Instead of answering the question, the woman waved her hand toward the sandwich and bottle of apple juice sitting on the tray. "Yest' pishchu."

Lainey stared at her in confusion.

"Eat... now," the woman said in a thick accent.

"I'm not hungry. Where's my mom?" repeated Lainey defiantly.

Irritated, the woman threw up her hands and then stormed out of the room. A few seconds later, she walked back in with a girl who looked about sixteen. She had long, brown hair pulled back in a ponytail, and blue eyeglasses. Lainey noticed that the girl held a book in one hand and a bottle of Diet Coke in another.

The woman said something to the teenager in Russian.

"Right," muttered the girl. Looking annoyed, she turned to Lainey. "My name is Tara. Who are you?"

"Lainey," she replied.

"Well, Lainey, Dina wants me to tell you the rules," she said in a bored tone. "So, listen up—"

Lainey frowned. "For what?"

"You know... For staying here."

"But, I don't want to stay here. I want to go home," said Lainey, her lip trembling.

"I know you do." She shrugged. "You just... can't."

Lainey didn't like that answer and began to cry.

Stiffening up, Tara moved closer to her. "Don't do that," she said, staring hard into Lainey's eyes. "Dina gets upset when kids cry. I don't want her to hurt you."

29

"I just want to go home! I don't want to be here," Lainey sobbed, tears rolling down her cheeks.

Dina walked over to the teenager and spoke sharply in Russian.

"Well, what did you expect? She wants to go home to her parents," Tara snapped back.

Glaring at her, Dina backhanded the teenager, who cried out.

Tara stumbled backward but caught herself before she fell to the floor.

Shocked, Lainey gasped in horror. She knew it was her fault. Crying, she begged Dina not to hurt Tara again. "I'm sorry. I'll be good! I promise!"

Glaring at Dina, Tara rubbed her reddened cheek and mumbled something under her breath.

Ignoring her, Dina crossed her arms under her chest and tapped her foot angrily on the floor. "Rules!"

Tara let out a ragged breath and looked at Lainey. "Rule number one is to do what they say. Rule number two is, don't try to escape. Rule number three is, don't piss any of them off. You'll regret it, and believe me, some of them enjoy causing pain."

Lainey shuddered, wondering who 'they' were. "They do?"

"Yeah. Oh, and rule number four is that if you fail to follow the first three rules, they'll kill you."

Lainey's eyes widened in shock. "Kill me?"

"Yeah, but, you're new, so they'll probably allow you a couple of strikes," continued the girl. "Still, if I were you, I wouldn't push it."

Dina's cell phone began to ring. She pulled it out of her pocket and walked out of the room.

Tara lowered her voice. "Oh, and be careful with Dina. If you get on her good side, you'll do okay. Get on her bad side, and you'll be hatin' life. I mean it."

"Who is she? Your sister?"

30

Tara's lips curled under. "God, no. She's the caretaker, I guess you could say," Tara replied, biting the side of her nail and staring at the doorway.

"Can we leave here?" she asked Tara.

She sighed. "No. I wish."

Lainey's eyes filled with tears. It sounded like Tara was a prisoner, too. "So, we can never go home?"

Before Tara could answer, Dina re-entered the room, still on the phone. She was talking rapidly to the person on the other end and looked frustrated.

"Not the kind of home you're used to," Tara replied grimly.

Dina hung up the phone and spoke sharply to Tara.

Nodding, the teenager looked at Lainey. "She wants you to eat, and if you behave, she said you can watch cartoons later. They have a bunch of Disney DVDs. Okay?"

"How can you understand what she's saying?"

"I've been with them for a long time," she said in a hollow voice, her eyes taking on a haunted look. "Anyway," She looked at Lainey again. "I can't understand everything. Only some things."

Dina spoke again in a softer tone.

"What did she say?" Lainey asked, noticing a frown spread across Tara's face.

"Another kid will be arriving soon," Tara told her.

Lainey tried asking more questions, but Dina interrupted and ordered Tara out of the room.

"Eat," Dina ordered, pointing at the plate of food.

Although she wasn't hungry, Lainey picked up the cold grilled cheese sandwich and took a bite. The woman watched her chew, and then waited for her to eat more of it. Lainey took another bite, too afraid to anger Dina after the way she'd attacked Tara.

"Now, drink," Dina said, waving her hand at the tray.

Lainey picked up the glass of juice and took a sip. She noticed
31

that it tasted funny. She told Dina, but the woman didn't seem to understand or care.

"Again," said Dina.

Lainey did, forcing the liquid down her throat. Although she didn't want to drink any more of it, Dina's temper scared her more than the horrible taste.

Satisfied, Dina left the room, locking the door behind her.

Alone again, she set down the sandwich and walked over to the window. She lifted the shade and was surprised to see that it was daylight.

Looking around, Lainey thought she might be on a farm. Down below her window was an old metal swing set and a picnic table where a man sat, smoking a cigarette and staring down at his phone. On the other side of the yard was an old red barn and a rusty tractor, overrun with weeds. Beyond that she saw nothing but grassy fields and tall trees.

Yawning, Lainey's eyelids grew heavy. She walked back over to the bed and crawled under the covers.

I want my Mommy, she thought, wishing she was in her mother's comforting arms. A few seconds later, she was sleeping and dreaming about Beth.

Chapter 6

Saturday

3:30 p.m.

Kurt

THE TWO MEN SAT quietly in a gray van, one of them playing a game on his phone, as the other absently flicked his Zippo lighter on and off. They were parked in front of the Cray Plaza and waiting for two females to walk out of the building. One of them, the older sister, was supposed to be in her early twenties. The other, their target, was around twelve.

"Are you sure your informant gave you the correct building?" mumbled Yury in a thick, Russian accent.

"Yeah," replied Kurt, looking up from his cell phone. "I know it's the right one. "Hawk saw them walk into the movie theater. It should be over soon."

Grunting, Yury shoved the lighter into his leather jacket. "I'm getting tired of waiting. Are you sure this one is even worth the trouble?"

"Oh, yeah. She's got the look. You know, blonde hair, blue eyes, innocent and sweet. Just how they like 'em. She's a money-maker. You'll see."

Yury sighed. "We shall see. We wait ten more minutes and if they don't show, we leave and try the mall."

"Whatever you say," he replied.

33

It was Yury's quarterly visit, making sure everything was running smoothly in the 'operation'. He didn't seem to understand that pulling kids off of the streets wasn't as easy as it was in Grozny. You needed to have patience, which was something Yury lacked. Fortunately, Kurt had it and more. He had employees willing to go the extra mile when it came to acquiring the children. Whether it was causing a distraction, befriending them on social media, or even cozying up to the parents, Kurt's group wasn't afraid to do whatever was needed. Especially, when they were paid so well for bringing him top-notch merchandise.

Kurt tilted his head to the right and then to the left, cracking his neck. It helped him relax. But only just a bit. Yury always put him on edge. He was from Grozny and not someone you wanted to piss off. Built like a wrestler, with an unpredictable temper, Yury was one intimidating son-of-a-bitch. Sometimes just the littlest things set him off, too. Kurt had once watched the Russian kill a guy with his bare hands for making a joke about his mother. Another time, he killed a prostitute's Pomeranian when it wouldn't stop barking at him. He was a cold-hearted prick, but the bastard had made Kurt and the others very rich. So, if Yury wanted to kill dogs or choke-out a few smart-asses, he'd get out of his way.

"We had a lot of bids on that last auction," Yury said, breaking the silence. "So, I've been thinking, we should increase supply to meet the demands of our customers."

He was talking about their private auction on the dark web. The products his organization sold were highly sought after, but illegal as shit. They ranged from snuff films, to stolen luxury cars, to women and children. Kurt's unit was responsible for acquiring model-quality American kids and were paid handsomely for it.

"We're already doing two auctions a week," said Kurt, the wheels in his head already spinning on how they could manage taking on more kids. They would need to start looking farther out.

34

Yury frowned. "Is this going to be a problem? If so, I will find someone else."

Kurt knew what that meant: do what was asked, or he, and his team, would lose more than just their jobs.

He forced a smile to his face. "Hell. No problem at all. How many are we talking?"

"Two per auction. Instead of one."

Kurt relaxed.

That wasn't so bad.

They already had the newest kid tucked away at the farmhouse and another beauty on the way. Unlike some of the other trafficking organizations, they took their time and did things the right way. They didn't keep a stable, which, in his opinion, was dangerous. It was asking for trouble. So they focused on the quality of their merchandise instead of quantity. And so far… it was paying off. "So, we're talking two this coming Friday?"

"Yes," said Yury, staring at a young, curvy woman walking by with her dog.

Still, Kurt had to wonder why the sudden change. In the past, Yury had said that selling more than one kid in an auction was allowing the buyers to relax. The customers knew if they were outbid on one child, they'd still have another to fall back on. But, if there was limited inventory available, the buyers went into a purchasing frenzy. They were like rabid dogs trying to get the very last morsel of food before anyone else could get to it.

"I thought you said you'd be losing money if you auctioned more than one a night?" Kurt asked.

"We're doing one girl. One boy. Two different customers," he replied, looking at Kurt as if he was a moron.

"Ah." That made sense. But that meant they'd need to get their hands on a boy by Friday. One that would please their elite bidders, who expected only the finest quality of merchandise.

Kurt sent a text to Hawk and then started the engine.

"We're leaving?" Yury asked, surprised. "What about the girl?"

"We're short on boys," Kurt said, pulling away from the curb. Besides, he hadn't liked the idea of taking the girl right off the street and killing the older sister, who was pregnant. He wasn't a complete monster.

"So, we go to the mall and search for one?"

"No. Too risky at this time of day. Besides, we need quality merchandise and don't want to grab just anyone."

Yury sighed. "So, what do you propose?"

Kurt lit a cigarette. "I sent Hawk a message. He'll find us someone."

"Good. Let's go and eat at that pizza joint on Seventh Street. Hunting always makes me hungry," Yury said.

"It closed down."

Yury swore. "Figures. Okay, let's get those little White Castle cheeseburgers. I like them."

"You sure you want to do that?" Kurt asked, remembering the last time Yury was in town. He'd spent most of the time in the bathroom after eating almost twenty of the greasy burgers.

"White Castles are good for the plumbing," he replied with a smirk. "You should eat some yourself. You look a little uptight."

Kurt didn't reply. Until Yury went back to Grozny, it would take more than a few sliders to make him relax.

Chapter 7

Beth

DETECTIVES SAMUELS AND Dubov showed up at Beth's house in the afternoon with more questions and a search warrant.

"I don't understand," Tom said. "Why would you need to search this place? She wasn't taken here."

"It's just standard procedure," Samuels said. "Nothing to get excited about. Also, we recommend that you both take polygraph tests."

"Why?" Beth asked, surprised and angry. "You honestly don't believe I had anything to do with this, do you?"

"Believe me, nobody is accusing you of anything. But, the sad truth is that in situations like this, the media isn't always your friend. In fact, if they suspect any kind of foul play on your part, they'll use it to their advantage to create a more interesting story," he replied.

"He's right. The media is heartless," said Dubov. "By taking a polygraph test, you're showing that you have nothing to hide and are willing to prove your innocence to the world."

"But they have the kidnapper on video," argued Tom. "We shouldn't have to show anyone anything."

"Because the kidnapper wore a disguise, everyone, aside from Beth, will be looked upon as a potential suspect," said Samuels.

37

"You're kidding?" said Tom angrily. "Even me?"

"Unfortunately, yes. But, if it makes you feel better, we don't think you're involved, Mr. Brown," Dubov replied.

"Thanks," he said dryly. Tom crossed his arms over his chest. "I'm not taking a damn polygraph, though. It's bullshit and I shouldn't have to prove my innocence to anyone. I mean, what reason would I have to kidnap my own daughter? It's not like I'm forbidden to see her or anything."

"Unfortunately, there are people out there willing to do anything for money," Samuels said. "The media knows it. The public knows it. Do yourself a favor and take the polygraph test, Mr. Brown."

Beth could tell that Tom wanted to punch Samuels in the face, and she couldn't exactly blame him. She understood his frustrations at being considered a suspect, but she also didn't want to make things any harder than they already were. And God forbid, she certainly didn't want anyone accusing him of being involved. "Just take one," Beth said wearily. "I will, too."

Tom looked at her. "No, Beth. I've heard stories about innocent people failing polygraphs. Look at that one guy who was falsely accused of killing his wife when it was found later that the BTK killer actually did it. That guy *failed* the test. Then there was the Green River Killer who passed the damn thing, and we all know he was a murderer. I refuse to take something that is fallible."

Dubov and Samuels glanced at each other.

"Look, anyone who believes that I kidnapped my own daughter can go to hell," said Tom. "I shouldn't have to defend myself. Especially since the kidnapper was caught on camera. Obviously, that piece of shit wasn't me."

"Maybe not, but there is one interesting detail about that video that is a little perplexing," Samuels said, scratching his chin.

Beth's eyes widened. "What do you mean?"

"Lainey was very comfortable around the man who took her. Not only did she let him get close enough to put something over her nose, but your daughter actually smiled at her abductor," he replied.

STILL, NOBODY HAD any answers, and Tom held firm in his decision to not take the polygraph test.

"That's fine," said Samuels. "And your choice. Don't say we didn't warn you, however."

Tom shrugged. "I doubt I have anything to worry about. Plus, I'm not hiding anything. If someone has a question, I'll be happy to answer it truthfully."

"And we appreciate that," said Samuels.

"For the record, Mr. Brown," said Dubov, "where were you last night at approximately 8:50 pm when your daughter went missing?"

"Just like I told you last night, I was at home. Alone," he replied icily. "Eating leftover pizza and watching an episode of *Game of Thrones*."

"Can you prove it?" Dubov asked.

Tom grunted. "Probably not."

"You live in an apartment complex, correct?" she said.

"Yes," he replied.

"Did you happen to pass anyone in the hallway or in the parking lot after Beth called you?" Samuels asked.

"No. Not that I recall. I was pretty shaken, though. I mean, who knows?" he said, getting agitated again. "Look, do I need to get a lawyer?"

"Actually, it wouldn't be a bad idea. Just in case," said Dubov.

"Oh, my God. Tom had nothing to do with this," Beth said

angrily. "Your questions are highly insulting and a waste of time. Why aren't you out there, looking for Lainey, instead of harassing him?"

"I'm sorry," Dubov said firmly. "But, our first priority is finding your daughter. Just like we said earlier, it's our job to check every angle and turn over every rock before we can rule out who is a suspect and who isn't. Feelings may get hurt in the process, but that's the way the cookie crumbles. We believe Lainey may have known the person. Is it like her to smile at strangers or allow them to get so close?"

"She might. I mean, maybe he said something funny or had a friendly face," said Tom wearily.

"Lainey is actually a very shy child," said Beth, frowning. "Especially around other adults. She might smile at a stranger, but even I have to admit that it *is* kind of strange how she didn't back away when he approached her the way he did. I wish I knew what had been going on in her mind."

"We all do," Tom mumbled.

"Why don't you give us a list of everyone Lainey knows, including teachers, friends, other parents, or anyone new who may have come in contact with her in the last few weeks," said Dubov.

"Okay," said Beth, walking over to the kitchen counter. She pulled out a notebook and a pen from one of the drawers and sat down at the kitchen table. As she began to write, the doorbell rang.

"I'll get it," Tom said, racing out of the kitchen.

Beth and the two detectives followed him into the living room. He opened the front door, and standing on the porch were Beth's father and stepmother.

"Hello, Tom," said William, a fit man with broad shoulders, cropped gray hair, and weathered skin. Standing next to him was Helen, a thin, attractive woman with bright blue eyes and perfectly coifed white hair.

40

"Hello, William. Helen. Come on in," Tom replied, moving out of the way.

William walked past him, to Beth. His eyes filled with tears. "Bethy," he choked, pulling her into his arms.

"Hi, Daddy," she said, blinking back her own tears. He hadn't called her Bethy in so long. "I'm so glad you're both here."

"Me, too," he said, hugging her tightly.

Beth closed her eyes, grateful for their arrival. Her father always made her feel safe, and somehow, having him there made her feel as if everything was going to be okay.

Helen walked over and joined in the hug. "Has there been any more news?" she asked, her own voice full of emotion as the three pulled apart.

"Unfortunately, no," Tom said, shoving his hands into his pockets. "Unless there is something the police are holding back on."

"No, Mr. Brown," said Samuels with a cool smile. "You know as much as we do."

Beth introduced Detectives Samuels and Dubov to her father and Helen.

"What can we do to help?" William asked. "Form a search party? Make posters? Just tell us and we'll do it."

"Posters would be good," Samuels replied as something caught his attention outside. He stepped closer to the large window that faced the street. "Looks like we have company."

Beth and the others looked outside. Three different news vans had pulled up to the house while the neighbors gawked in surprise.

"Good. We need to get Lainey's picture on television so the public can help find her," said William, watching as reporters and camera crews piled out of the vehicles.

"Yes," agreed Samuels. "Which is why we should also discuss what you should talk about on camera."

41

AN HOUR LATER, Tom and Beth stood in front of the reporters and gave their speech, which was mainly directed toward the kidnappers. They talked about Lainey and how much she meant to them while begging for her safe return. When they were finished with their statements, the reporters began asking questions, and that's when Detective Samuels stepped in. He gave a few more details of the case to the press and then the Browns were ushered back into the house.

"What do we do now?" asked Beth when they were back in the living room.

The detectives gave her some pamphlets to read and advised the couple to contact the National Center for Missing and Exploited Children for extra support and assistance while they continued to search for Lainey.

"They have a lot of resources to help families cope with situations like this," Detective Dubov said.

"Thanks," said Tom, peering over Beth's shoulder at the pamphlets while she searched through them.

"Do you have any suspects at all?" William asked.

"Unfortunately, not yet," Samuels said. "We're working on it, though."

"Have any recent sex offenders been released from jail?" Helen asked.

William cringed, but didn't say anything.

"Not recently, but we are certainly checking on offenders in that area and surrounding neighborhoods," Dubov replied.

Beth's phone rang. She saw it was Mike, and sighed in relief.

"I'm at the airport. I'm going to stop at my place quickly and then head over," he told her. "Have you learned anything new about Lainey yet?"

42

"No, unfortunately," she said sadly.

Mike sighed. "Don't worry, Beth. I'm sure they'll find her."

Beth had learned that each hour Lainey stayed missing meant the chances of finding her became slimmer, but she refused to accept it. Tears filled her eyes again. "I hope so."

"Has anyone called about a ransom?"

"No," she replied, although if the kidnapping was about money, at least it would offer her more hope of getting Lainey back. Even if they had to borrow money from her father. He'd already offered to lend her whatever was needed.

"Is Tom with you?"

"Yes," she replied, looking over at her ex, who was still talking with the police.

"Are you sure he didn't have anything to do with it?"

Beth wiped the moisture from under her eyes. *Why was everyone asking about Tom being involved?* "He would never do something like that," she said in a low voice.

"I just…" he sighed, "was thinking that… he *is* a gambler. I mean, what if he owed a large sum of money to some bookie and decided that a ransom was the only way to go?"

"Now that makes no sense at all," Beth said, the idea of Tom being involved sounding ludicrous. She would know if her ex-husband was capable of that, and Tom wasn't. "Besides, I have no money and he knows that."

"Maybe not, but your parents do, and I'm not exactly struggling with finances."

Beth knew Mike and his brother Mitch were very well off. He lived in an expensive house in Wayzata, drove a Porsche, and owned a large boat. Although she hadn't yet been on it, she'd seen pictures of his Carver and knew it cost more than her home.

Beth stepped out of the living room and into the kitchen for privacy. "Mike, he would never do this. I know Tom. He might

43

Looking for Lainey   Kristen Middleton

have a gambling problem, but he'd never put his own daughter in danger or use her to pay a gambling debt."

"Even in a matter of life or death? If he owed the wrong people money, I'm pretty sure they wouldn't take an IOU."

"He didn't do this," she said firmly.

"Okay," he replied. "You know him better than anyone, I guess. Or, at least you must have thought you did before marrying him."

She couldn't argue that point. If she'd known how bad Tom's gambling habit had been, she might not have married him in the first place. Still, kidnapping his own child and thinking he could get away with it? That wasn't Tom. Besides, in her own way, she still loved the man, and the thought of him doing something so sinister wasn't anything she wanted to consider.

"Okay, babe. My ride is here," Mike said. "I'll see you soon."

They hung up and Beth returned to the living room. She stared at Tom as he spoke to Samuels and found that although she'd protested his innocence, she was beginning to wonder why he was being so pig-headed about the lie detector test.

44

Chapter 8

Four Days Later

Carissa

CARISSA JONES FOLLOWED the hostess to the booth, where Dustin Frazer was seated and waiting for her. Noticing her arrival, he stood up.

Carissa thanked the woman and sat down across from him. She breathed in the familiar scent of his cologne and realized how much she'd missed it. Along with the man who still took her breath away.

"Hi, gorgeous," Dustin said, sitting back down. "It's great seeing you again."

"You, too," she replied, noticing the tiredness in his eyes and the new sprinkle of gray in his sideburns. It had been a few months since they'd last seen each other, and his appearance concerned her. He was only thirty-four and his job as a private detective was definitely affecting his health. But, it shouldn't have been a surprise to her. Dustin threw himself into his work and some of his cases were nasty. Including the one he wanted to talk to her about.

Dustin grinned. "I know. You don't have to say it," he said, as if reading her mind. "I look like shit."

"Shit? Not at all," she said honestly.

Even as tired as he looked, Dustin was still the most attractive man in the room. In any room, as far as she was concerned. She'd missed looking into those gray-blue eyes. Running her hands through his curly black hair. And seeing his adorable dimples, which still made her swoon. Carissa was just glad he wasn't the psychic in the booth. He'd know that just seeing him made her heart ache.

"You look like you haven't slept in a while, though," she said to him.

"The bed is cold without you," he said in a low voice. "What can I say?"

They'd ended their relationship on a bad note and it had nothing to do with lack of love or desire. The problem had been Dustin's unwillingness to take her psychic premonitions seriously. At least when they involved him. In a couple of her visions, she'd seen him get shot and had implored Dustin to make a career change. Stubbornly, he refused to even consider it. That had started a wave of arguments, and eventually, it ended their relationship. But Carissa knew he still had feelings for her, as she did for him. Unfortunately, his passion for his job overrode everything else, even his love life. Part of her understood, especially since he was driven by the fact that his sister had been abducted many years ago and never found. He'd spent most of his career trying to find answers, which even Carissa couldn't provide. Now, after leaving a career in law enforcement, he was a private investigator and specialized in missing persons.

"Not fair. And we're not here to talk about us, if I remember correctly."

He sighed. "No. But, for the record, I miss you."

Their eyes met and she smiled. "I know."

They both laughed.

46

The waitress took that moment to check on the couple. Carissa ordered an iced tea and Dustin, a beer. When they were left alone again, she asked him about the case.

Dustin pulled out a manila folder. He took out a picture of the missing girl and told her everything he knew about the investigation.

"The police haven't had any luck, and that's why Lainey's grandfather, William McKenzie, called me."

"And you haven't made much progress, either," she said, staring down at the photo. Lainey reminded her a lot of Chloe, the last girl she'd helped locate, with her long, blonde hair and blue eyes, only a little older.

"No."

She closed her eyes. Carissa had asked Dustin not to tell her too much so she could feel out the case with an open mind. All she really knew was that the girl had been taken from a Walmart while shopping with her mother.

"Do you think she's alive?" he asked softly, breaking the silence after several seconds.

"Yes," replied Carissa, feeling it in her gut. "She's… valuable to her kidnappers."

"Trafficking?"

She opened her eyes. "I think so."

"Did you happen to catch the news about the missing eleven-year-old boy? Sammy Johnson?"

"No. When did he go missing?" she asked, saddened to hear that another child was missing.

"Last night. Around seven-thirty. Apparently, he was last seen leaving a friend's house on foot. He never made it home."

News like this made her sick to her stomach. Children were so innocent and the world was filled with such wicked, wicked people.

Most of them having been victims themselves at one point, repeating patterns. "So, there weren't any witnesses?"

"No."

Carissa sighed.

"Do you think it's related to Lainey's case?"

She frowned. "To tell you the truth, I'm drawing a blank. Where did he disappear?"

"By Lake Calhoun."

Carissa chewed on her lower lip. "I just… Unfortunately, I'm having a hard time concentrating here." She put the photo back into the folder. "It's too hectic in the restaurant."

Dustin's eyes twinkled. "We could go back to my place. Turn off the lights. Put on some soft music. Hell, I'd even be willing to give you a massage if it will help you relax more,"

"Yeah, I bet," she said with a small smile. "I think we should go to where Lainey was taken, Walmart, and the sooner, the better. Maybe something will come to me about Sammy, too."

His face became serious again. "Okay. Let's just grab a quick bite and head over there. I haven't eaten since yesterday."

"Why does that not surprise me? You need to start taking better care of yourself."

"This case has made me lose my appetite," he said, staring down at the menu.

"I can imagine." Carissa opened up her menu and decided on a cup of chili and a grilled cheese sandwich. It was supposed to snow and the case was already chilling her to the bone. She needed warmth and comfort food. "So, did you mention to Lainey's family that you were seeking advice from a psychic?"

"Not yet. I'm not sure how they'll react. I figured if you are able to pick up something important—something that could help—I'd go from there."

"I understand." Carissa was used to skeptics and cynics. Most people thought she was a fraud or a nut-job. Hell, sometimes she wondered if she was a little crazy. But there was no denying her visions or dreams. Especially, when they came true.

The waitress returned with their drinks and they ordered food.

"How did things go up north?" he asked her. "You found that missing girl, right?"

"Yes. Unfortunately, he killed another child, though, and got away. It was a mess." Carissa told him what had happened in Castle Danger.

"Don't be so hard on yourself. You did what you could and saved Chloe's life. There's no shame in that. You should be proud of yourself."

Carissa's smile was humble. "I know. I just hope he doesn't go after her again."

"Do you think he will?"

"I really don't know." She sighed. "It's so frustrating… only getting bits and pieces of things. I mean, I really don't have a clue whether or not he's going to go after her again. But I'm pretty sure he is going to keep looking for the daughter he lost. Which means more victims. It's upsetting. I wish he hadn't gotten away."

"I'm sure. You haven't had any other premonitions about the guy?"

She shook her head. "Nothing. Although, it's only been a few days. Anyway, ever since you called me, I keep thinking about Lainey and she's the priority at the moment." Carissa opened up the folder and stared down at the picture again. Frowning, she looked at Dustin.

"What is it?"

"I almost feel like her abductor isn't the real threat."

He frowned. "What do you mean?"

Carissa stared off into space and was silent for a few seconds. She was suddenly struck with a premonition that made her sick to her stomach. Carissa closed her eyes to try and see more. "Her captor isn't going to hurt her, but… someone else will. Someone who enjoys…" She envisioned a man in a tuxedo. She couldn't see his face, but noticed something that made her shudder.

"What is it?" Dustin asked, touching her hand.

She opened up her eyes. "I saw a wedding dress," Carissa said grimly. "On Lainey."

Chapter 9

Beth

"BETH, YOU HAVE to eat something," William said, standing in her bedroom doorway. He looked around the dark room and fought the urge to open up her blinds and let in the afternoon sunshine. "You're not doing Lainey any favors by starving yourself."

She stared blindly at the television screen. "I'm not hungry." Beth raised the remote control and began flipping through the channels. She wasn't interested in watching TV, but needed constant distraction to keep her sane.

William sighed and walked into the room. "I know you're depressed and hurting. We're *all* hurting. But, you have to stay strong for her and not give up."

Beth knew he was right, but her heart ached so damn badly. She could feel herself descending into deep despair and it wasn't just depressing. It was exhausting. Even the thought of taking a shower seemed like too much work. Plus, with every hour she didn't hear back from the police, the feeling of hopelessness debilitated her even more. If that wasn't bad enough, Mike was heading out of town again, this time to view artwork from a painter for an upcoming show he was hosting. She understood that the world needed to go on, but for her, it couldn't. Not without Lainey.

"Hey, I know. Why don't we go out and hang more fliers?" he said, sitting down on the corner of the bed. "It will do you good to get out of the house, and who knows, maybe the kidnappers have gotten less cautious with her? Someone might recognize Lainey from a gas station or a store. Maybe even a McDonald's."

She didn't say anything.

William sighed. "Okay, someone has to say it—stop feeling sorry for yourself. Lainey isn't going to be found unless we all work together to bring her home. That means getting out of this house and doing something. Even if it's just hanging up more damn posters."

Beth looked at him. She knew he was right, even though the last thing she felt like doing was getting out of bed. "Where do you propose we hang them? The kidnappers might not even be in the Twin Cities anymore."

He squeezed her foot. "It doesn't matter. We just need to do something, and hiding in here isn't helping."

Beth turned off the television. He had a point. And she *was* feeling sorry for herself, which now made her feel ashamed. "I'll go take a shower."

Relief flooded his face. He smiled. "Now we're talking. By the way, Tom is on his way over again."

She nodded.

He and her father had finally put aside their differences. At least for the time being. Unlike her, Tom was harassing Samuels every day about updates and had even called some of the local radio stations, asking them to spread the news about Lainey. He'd also put together a meeting at Lainey's elementary school, to let parents know what they could do to help, as well as how to protect their own children. Beth was thankful for his determination and knew she should be doing the same things, but couldn't seem to find the energy. It had gotten so bad that Mike had even suggested anti-depressants.

"Drugs aren't going to bring her back," she'd argued.

"No, but they might bring you back."

Beth had brushed his advice off, knowing that it left him frustrated. But she didn't care. She knew there was no way he could completely understand the turmoil she was going through. Although he loved Lainey, it wasn't his flesh and blood who'd been kidnapped.

William told her he'd keep an eye out for Tom and then walked out of the bedroom.

Beth dragged herself out of the bed, grabbed a towel, and took a shower. As the water slid down her head, she wept some more. Although she'd spent the last few days crying, it seemed like her tears were never-ending. All Beth could think about was Lainey. What she had to be going through. And… how her mother had failed her.

AFTER THE SHOWER, Beth threw on a pair of jeans and a sweatshirt, noting that her clothes were beginning to hang on her. Her father was obviously right. She needed to eat, at least for Lainey's sake.

When Beth finally made it to the kitchen, she saw that Tom and her father were seated at the table and in deep conversation.

"Hi, Beth," Tom said, looking up at her.

"Hi." She walked over to the coffee machine and proceeded to make herself a cup.

"Have you told Beth yet?" Tom asked William.

Beth looked over her shoulder. "Told me what?"

"I hired a private investigator a couple days ago. To see if he could help find Lainey," said William.

53

Surprised, she walked over to the table. Like Tom, she felt as if the police weren't doing enough, so this was good news. "Really? Has he found out anything yet?"

"No, unfortunately. But he believes the men who took Lainey were definitely traffickers. In fact, I just got off the phone with him while you were in the shower," William said, before taking a sip of coffee.

Beth sighed. If it really was sex-trafficking, God forbid, then they'd need nothing short of a miracle to find Lainey. She'd been doing some research and knew that right now, her daughter could be anywhere in or out of the country. "Do you honestly think he'll have a better chance of finding her than the police?"

"He's focused on finding her, and nobody else. Plus, he used to be a cop. I have to believe that if anyone can find her, it's Dustin. Although, I'm starting to question his methods," William replied with a funny smile.

"What do you mean?" Tom asked.

"He has this female psychic friend who has helped him locate children in the past. He spoke with her and she's agreed to help," William said.

Tom sighed and ran a hand over his face. "Oh, here we go. And how much is that going to cost?"

William shrugged. "He didn't say. I'm pretty sure it's included in the fees I'm paying him. At least, it better be."

"You said this woman helped find other missing children?" Beth asked, feeling more awake than she had in days. Unlike Tom and her father, she believed there actually were gifted psychics, and if one of them could possibly help find Lainey, she was all for it. "What's her name?"

"He didn't mention it, but they were headed over to Walmart when we last spoke," her father replied.

54

"We should go there, too," said Beth, adrenalized and feeling a sudden new spark of hope. "Can you call him back and let him know that we're also on our way?"

"If you want to, sure," William replied, taking out his phone. "You'd better eat something, though. You look like your clothes are about to slide right off of you."

Beth opened up the cupboard and grabbed a granola bar. "Is this better?"

"It will have to do," William said with a disapproving look. "For now. I guess."

She tore open the wrapper. "I'm going to get my purse. I'll meet you outside. Hi, Helen," Beth said, passing her on her way out of the kitchen.

"Hi, dear. What's going on?" she asked William and Tom. William explained.

"A psychic? Can I come, too?" Helen asked, looking intrigued.

"If you want to," William replied. "But you know how I feel about psychics. I think involving her is a waste of time."

"Maybe, but I think it's important to explore all options in trying to locate Lainey," she replied. "And… it's better than sitting around here and twiddling our thumbs."

"She has a point," said Tom, standing up and pulling out the car keys from his pocket. "Although, this woman better not put any false ideas into Beth's head."

"I think we'll know soon enough if this psychic is a total flake," William replied with a smirk. "I just hope she doesn't send us all on a wild goose chase."

Chapter 10

Carissa

THEY TOOK DUSTIN'S PICKUP to Walmart. Just as they were pulling into a parking spot, he received a phone call from Lainey's grandfather.

"It looks like the family is going to meet us here," he told Carissa after the conversation, shoving his phone back into his jacket pocket.

"Good idea," she replied, staring at the busy store. Even though the abduction had occurred later in the evening, it was shocking that nobody had noticed anything unusual. But then again, people were usually in a hurry, especially at that time of night, or had their eyes glued to their phones.

"You've been quiet. Are you picking up anything yet from the land of 'Supernatural'?" he asked with a little smile.

"No," she said with a sigh. "I was just thinking about how gutsy the kidnappers were. Taking a child out of a busy store like this. She was drugged, right?"

He nodded. "And it's believed that Lainey might have known the abductor."

"Hmm."

It would make sense. That's how he would have been able to get close enough to use chloroform, too, which was what she suspected.

They got out of Dustin's truck and headed inside. Although it was earlier in the day, it was still rather busy with people shopping for the holidays, and Carissa felt even more pressured to help return Lainey. She couldn't imagine what it would be like to lose a child, especially around this time of the year. Thanksgiving and Christmas would never be the same for her parents. Of course, nothing would.

When they arrived at the aisle where Lainey had been kidnapped, Carissa was immediately drawn to the rows of Barbie dolls. She picked up one of the boxes and studied it.

"What is it?" Dustin asked quietly.

She looked at him, her eyes sparkling. "Lainey wanted this doll. Badly."

He nodded. "William mentioned she'd been pining for a doll and had gotten mad at Beth because she refused to buy it for her. Pretty classic exchange between parent and child in the toy department."

"Yes."

Relieved that she was picking up something significant, Carissa's heart quickened. She closed her eyes and concentrated.

"So, Lainey stomped back here and was putting the doll away when the kidnapper approached her."

"Yeah."

"I also feel that she definitely knew this man." Beth was silent for a while. After a few seconds, she opened up her eyes.

"What?"

She shook her head, frustrated. "Sorry. I'm drawing more blanks again. I'm probably trying too hard."

"It's okay. Take your time."

57

Beth put the doll back onto the shelf and looked up toward the ceiling. She knew the store had to have hidden cameras everywhere. "Have you seen the surveillance videos?"

"No. I tried getting the store manager to show them to me yesterday, but he was busy and not very helpful."

"Maybe Lainey's parents can talk him into letting us see them?"

"That would be nice."

She looked around the aisle. "If you don't mind, I'm going to spend some more time here and see if anything else comes to me."

"No problem. I'll grab a cup of coffee from the snack bar. Would you like something to drink?"

"Sure. Thank you. Coffee sounds good."

Dustin smiled. "Let me guess—an iced caramel frappe?"

Carissa grinned back at him. "You know what I like."

He winked. "I'll be back."

She watched Dustin walk away and then turned back toward the rows of dolls. "Please. Give me something," she whispered, closing her eyes again.

AS DUSTIN STOOD in line for the coffee, his thoughts were on Carissa. He had missed the hell out of the woman, and seeing her was difficult. If anything, she looked more beautiful than ever. Her auburn hair had gotten longer and she'd put on a couple of pounds, which was good, considering the last time they'd seen each other, Carissa had looked almost… gaunt. But now her face had filled out a little, and her green eyes were lively again.

He wondered if she'd met someone.

The thought made his stomach twist. Although he wanted her to be happy, he was selfish and knew it. He loved her and the thought of any other guy in her life would never sit well. If only she wasn't so stubborn. He understood why she was anxious about his job, but he couldn't give it up. And Carissa knew why.

Dustin thought about his younger sister, Taylor, who'd been abducted when she was nine years old. She'd disappeared while riding her bike home for dinner. The police found it on the side of a dirt road, but there'd been no sign of Taylor and no witnesses. It had destroyed their parents and he'd felt like the worst brother in the world. Especially since Dustin had been asked to chaperone Taylor from her friend, Jenny's house. But he'd talked his way out of it, claiming he'd had an important test to study for. Although it had been partially true, he'd simply been too damn lazy.

Afterward, guilt and shame had eaten him up inside. It had gotten so bad that at one point, he'd even contemplated suicide. But watching his parents drink themselves to death because of their own demons had triggered something deep inside of him. He finally realized that suicide wouldn't bring his sister back, but he could dedicate his life to her. Instead of wallowing in guilt and self-pity, he decided to get into law enforcement in hopes of seeking some kind of justice for Taylor and other missing kids. Unfortunately, he never did find out who'd kidnapped his sister, and even Carissa couldn't give him the kind of answers he needed.

"Sir, what can I get for you?" the clerk asked, snapping him out of his thoughts.

"Oh, sorry," Dustin said, stepping forward. He ordered the coffees, paid for them, and then headed back toward the toy department. On his way, he met up with Lainey's family. William made the introductions, and then they accompanied him back to the Barbie aisle.

"Did you hear about the missing boy?" William asked as they were walking through the store.

Dustin sighed. "Yeah. I saw the Amber Alert."

"The police aren't sure if the cases are related, because Sammy's a boy and three years older," he said. A look of disgust crossed his face. "There sure are a lot of crazies out there."

"Yeah, there certainly are," he replied, thinking of his sister again and all the other missing children. He wanted kids himself one day, but the truth was, the world scared the hell out of him.

"So, Mr. Frazer, Dad mentioned that your psychic friend has helped locate other children?" Beth asked him.

"Call me Dustin, please. And yes, in fact, she just helped find a little girl in Two Harbors last weekend," he replied.

Beth's face brightened. "Really? How did she get involved with that?"

"Carissa mentioned that she'd been drawn to Duluth even before the child went missing. She'd had some dreams and premonitions. Unfortunately, the kidnapper still took the girl, but Carissa helped her escape and was able to return her to her family," Dustin said.

"I heard something about that on the news," William said, looking impressed. "That was your psychic friend, huh? Carissa, you said?"

"Yes. Carissa Jones," Dustin replied. "And, she has located other kids, too. But, I have to tell you that her premonitions aren't controllable. She's going to do what she can to help, but I don't want to give you any false hope."

"That's understandable," Beth said. "We'll take what we can get."

"If there's one thing I know about Carissa, she'll do her best to help find Lainey, though. She loves children," Dustin replied as they rounded the corner and walked toward the doll aisle.

"This isn't going to cost extra, is it?" William asked through the side of his mouth.

Helen elbowed him.

60

Dustin bit back a smile. "Don't worry. She doesn't expect payment. She just wants to do the right thing and find your daughter."

"I don't care if there's a cost or not," Beth said. "I just want Lainey back, and if she finds her, I'll owe her for the rest of my life."

Tom, who'd been listening quietly, took her hand. "We both will," he said quietly.

Chapter 11

Lainey

"COME," DINA ORDERED. Today she was dressed in black leggings and a sparkly off-the-shoulder white sweater. She had on makeup and her hair fell softly over her shoulders.

Lainey stiffened up. "Why?"

"Come," repeated Dina, more sternly this time.

Remembering Tara's warnings, Lainey got out of the bed and timidly walked over to her. She hadn't been able to leave the bedroom since she'd arrived and wondered what was happening.

Dina mumbled something under her breath and then grabbed Lainey's hand. She pulled her out of the bedroom and down the hallway, to a long staircase. Dina's heels clicked loudly on the wood as they descended the steps.

"Where are you taking her?" called a voice.

Lainey looked up to see Tara staring down at them, a funny expression on her face.

Dina ignored the teenager.

"Dina!" called Tara angrily. "What's going on?"

Reaching the bottom of the staircase, the older woman turned and spoke to Tara in Russian.

"Oh," Tara replied, her face falling. "Already?"

"Yes. This isn't hotel," said Dina, pursing her lips.

62

Lainey's heart skipped a beat.

What did that mean?

Were they sending her somewhere?

"Am I going home?" Lainey asked.

Dina smirked. "Soon, yes. *New* home."

Her eyes filled with tears. "I don't want to go to a new home. I want my old one."

Dina ignored her. "Come," she said, trying to pull her forward.

"But, I don't want to!" cried Lainey shrilly.

Growling in the back of her throat, Dina whirled around. "Rules. Don't forget," she said coldly.

"Please, I just want to go home!" Lainey begged, trying to pull her hand out of Dina's.

The woman's face turned red. "Stop this. Now."

Lainey twisted her wrist and managed to break free. She backed away. "I want my mom!"

Furious, Dina grabbed her by the arm and slapped her across the face.

Lainey cried out in pain. She covered her cheek and began to sob.

Tara rushed down the staircase. "Dina, what the hell? She's just a little girl. You don't have to be such a bitch."

"Careful," Dina said, glaring at her. She shook her finger at Tara. "Or… you'll be next."

A man suddenly appeared in the foyer. "What's going on out here?"

"Dina slapped Lainey," Tara said, still glaring at the other woman.

Letting out a weary sigh, he turned to Dina. "Why?"

Dina raised her chin defiantly. "Misbehaving."

"She just asked to go home," Tara snapped. "That's not misbehaving. It's being human. Remember what that's like, Dina?"

She grunted and looked away.

The man leaned down and touched Lainey on the shoulder. "Are you okay, sweetheart? Let me see your face."

Surprised at the stranger's kindness, Lainey removed her hand from her cheek and stared at the man. He was nice looking with blonde hair, soft brown eyes, and a friendly smile.

"You'll be fine. So, you're Lainey? My name is Kurt, by the way," he murmured, touching her cheek gently. "Does that hurt?"

Lainey flinched and backed away from the man. She'd heard all about Kurt from Tara. He'd kidnapped her when she was eleven and had taken pictures of her. Naked ones.

Noticing the look of distaste on Lainey's face, Kurt's smile faltered. He stood up straight and turned to Dina. "Hands off. We need to take some pictures. You know that."

Dina sighed. "Fine."

He stared at her quietly for a few seconds. "You look lovely this evening," Kurt said in a warmer voice.

Dina's eyes lit up and she smiled. "Maybe... we have dinner tonight?"

"I don't think it's going to happen. There's too much going on," Kurt replied. "Yury is in town."

Dina's smile fell. "I know."

"Tell you what, when he leaves I'll take you someplace special," Kurt said, tilting his head. "Okay?"

She nodded.

Kurt looked around. "Speaking of Yury, he's waiting to see both kids. Where's the boy?"

Lainey's eyes widened. She didn't know there was a boy in the house.

"Sleeping," said Tara. "I just checked on him."

"Must be because of the chloroform," Kurt said.

Tara's eyes narrowed. "Maybe he was given too much."

64

Kurt shook his head. "I doubt it. Hawk knows what he's doing. Dina, go and get him, will you?"

Dina groaned. "Why can't Tara?"

"Because I asked you," he said sternly.

Grumbling under her breath, Dina stomped upstairs and disappeared.

"I'm going into the kitchen. Take her into the parlor," Kurt said, walking away.

Tara sighed and turned to Lainey. "Come on."

"I'm scared," murmured Lainey. "Who is Yury?"

"A creep, but at least he doesn't like touching kids." Tara grabbed Lainey's hand and gave her a reassuring squeeze.

That didn't make her feel much better. "Who's Dina going to get?" Lainey asked.

"A boy named Sammy," she replied as they began walking down the hallway.

"Was he kidnapped, too?"

She nodded.

When they entered the parlor, Lainey saw a muscular, bald man waiting for them. He wore a blue silk shirt and a chunky gold chain around his neck.

"Ah, yes," Yury said, nodding in approval when he saw Lainey. "You are a lovely little thing, aren't you?"

Something about the way he looked at her made Lainey's skin crawl. She swallowed the lump in her throat and looked away.

Yury took out a cigarette and lit it. "Where is the other one?"

"Dina went to get him," Tara replied.

"Ah. Good. Well, you're growing up nicely," he said, blowing out a cloud of smoke. His eyes traveled up and down Tara's figure. "I think we might have better use for you than babysitting. Much better."

Her eyes widened in alarm. "But, Kurt promised that I didn't have to do anything—"

Yury snorted. "Kurt? He can't promise anything. *I'm* in charge."

"But," Tara looked like she was going to be sick, "I've done everything that's been asked of me. He promised."

"No buts," he scowled. "You'll do what I say you'll do. End of discussion."

Kurt walked into the parlor with two beers. "What's going on?" he asked, handing one of the bottles to Yury.

"Tara forgot her place," Yury replied, twisting the cap off the beer. "I had to remind her of where it is."

Kurt glanced at Tara. "I'm sure Tara meant no disrespect. Right?"

"No," she mumbled, a sullen look on her face.

"I want her doing movies now," Yury said, sitting back in the sofa. He smirked. "In fact, I think I will bring her back to Grozny with me."

Tara gasped. "No. No. Please," she said, her eyes filling with tears. Tara looked at Kurt. "You said if I was good, I could watch the kids. I've done everything you asked."

"Why don't we talk about this later?" Kurt said, looking uncomfortable. "Right now, we should focus on the upcoming auction."

Although she didn't know what they were talking about, Lainey's stomach filled with dread.

"Yes. Good idea. How much do you think we can get for this little one?" Yury said, nodding toward Lainey.

"Quite a bit, I'm hoping," Kurt replied, staring at her. "Look at how much we got for the last little blondie. And this one looks almost like a china doll."

66

Realizing they were talking about selling her, Lainey rushed over to Tara and threw her arms around her waist. "Tara, I'm scared."

"Hey, it's okay," Tara whispered, hugging her back. "Everything will be fine."

"See. This is why we need Tara," Kurt said before taking a swig of beer. "They trust her and she calms them down."

Lainey knew it was more than that. Tara had brought her snacks and even held her a few times while Lainey cried. Tara actually cared about her. And she cared about Tara.

Yury waved his hand. "Eh, Dina can do that, too."

Kurt chuckled. "Dina? She's as warm as an iceberg."

Just then, Dina stepped into the parlor, dragging a boy who appeared to be a little older than Lainey.

"Quit," Dina hissed, struggling with Sammy.

"I want to go home!" he hollered, fighting to get away from her. He tried uncurling Dina's fingers from his wrist. "Let me go!"

"Enough!" barked Yury. He got up and stepped over to the boy. "Now you listen here. If you don't stop this foolishness, I will kill your parents. Your pets. Your friends. Anyone and everyone you love. I will make sure they suffer like you can't even imagine."

The boy stared up at him in frozen terror.

"You understand?" Yury said, his eyes bugging out. He grabbed his arm. "I'm not joking."

Trembling, the boy nodded.

Yury let go of the child and looked at Kurt. "See. You don't need to coddle these kids. They just need to know the rules and that if they don't follow them," he looked at Sammy again, "people they care about will suffer horribly for their actions."

Lainey shivered. Yury scared her more than anyone in the house. He was like the bad men in the movies. The ones who killed people. Only, he was real and not an actor.

67

Yury began unbuttoning his sleeve. "Now, you will both sit still and behave so we can take your pictures. You got it?"

Both Lainey and Sammy nodded.

Smiling, he looked at Kurt. "And you didn't think I was good with children. You see? These kids are not stupid. They are smart. They respect fear. Fear is how you get things done. And nobody…" he winked, "does fear better than me."

Chapter 12

Carissa

WHEN DUSTIN AND Lainey's family met up with Carissa, they found her standing next to a row of Barbies, her eyes closed, and hands resting on the shelf. Customers quietly walked by with questioning and amused expressions on their faces, but gave her space.

"That must be her," Helen murmured.

He smiled. "By golly, Helen." William put his arm around her shoulders. "You never mentioned that you were clairvoyant, too."

"Oh, you…" she elbowed him in the ribcage.

Smiling at the older couple's banter, Carissa opened her eyes and turned toward Dustin, who made the introductions.

"Your daughter looks just like you," she said to Beth, who had honey-blonde hair and light blue eyes. Makeup-less and with her hair in a ponytail, she looked more like a high school student than a mother approaching thirty.

Beth smiled sadly. "People tell us that all the time."

Tom put his arm around her shoulders. "As you can see, Lainey's beauty was passed down from Beth. Thank goodness," he said with a smile.

69

Beth stiffened at his touch. "Come on now. You're not exactly the Ugly Duckling. Lainey thinks you're the most handsome man in the world," she said.

Tom still loves her, Carissa thought. She knew they were divorced, but it was obvious he wasn't happy with the situation.

"She should see me now," he replied sadly.

Tom was about a foot taller than Beth, with brown hair, thick eyebrows, and a few days' growth of beard. Although he looked weary, Carissa thought he was far from ugly.

Pulling away from him, Beth walked over to the Barbie dolls. "This is the one she wanted," she said, picking up a box.

"That's what I thought," Carissa said. "I was drawn to her."

Beth's eyes widened. "Really?"

She nodded.

"So, have you come up with anything?" Dustin asked, handing her the frappe.

"She was taken by someone she knew and was surprised to see him here," Carissa said before taking a sip of coffee.

"That's what the police thought as well. Do you know who he is or how she knows him?" Beth asked, looking hopeful.

Carissa gave her an apologetic look. "I'm sorry. I don't. Not yet, at least."

"At least she's honest about not knowing," muttered Tom.

Carissa looked at him. "Actually, I do know certain things about the kidnapper, just not a name or face. He's a man in his thirties. He's been around your daughter quite a bit and very familiar to her."

Everyone stared at her, stunned.

"Could it be someone from her school?" Beth asked.

Carissa nodded. "Yes. It's very possible. He could also be a coach or… a friend's father."

70

"Is there anything more you can tell us?" Beth asked, searching her face. "Like, has she been harmed?"

Carissa felt that Beth's daughter wasn't hurt, yet, but was definitely in grave danger.

"I don't feel as if she's been hurt. But, I'm pretty sure the group who has Lainey is involved with child trafficking. I think…" Carissa didn't want to say the words, but knew she had to. "I think they plan on selling her. And soon."

Beth stared at her in horror.

"Dear God," Helen said, placing a hand on her chest. "Who could sell a child? What kind of monsters are they?"

"The worst, apparently. Can you help us find her before that happens?" William asked in a gruff voice.

"I'm going to try my very best." Carissa looked at Dustin. "Are you still friends with Jeremy?"

His face lit up. "Yes." Dustin pulled out his phone. "I'll give him a call. I can't believe I didn't think about him before."

"Who's Jeremy?" Tom asked.

"He used to work for the government. Anyway, he's the best hacker I've ever met and knows how to maneuver around the dark web," Dustin said. "Hopefully, he can help us."

"What's the dark web?" Beth asked.

"It's a haven for criminal activity. You need special software to access it, and most people aren't aware it even exists," Dustin explained.

"So, you think whoever took Lainey might know something about it on this 'dark web'?" William asked, looking intrigued.

"It's possible," Dustin said.

"There are a lot of bad things to be found on there. And most of the users use a program called Tor to hide their I.P. addresses so they can browse or conduct business anonymously," Carissa said. Jeremy had helped with another case and had educated her on both

71

Tor and the dark web. "Like pedophiles and people who are willing to exploit children for money."

"Wow, my skin feels like it's crawling just hearing about it," Beth replied with a grimace.

Dustin nodded. "There's a lot of disturbing things going on there. People sell drugs. Weapons. Illegal pornography. Woman and children. And, because of Tor, it makes it that much easier for the sleaze-balls to remain anonymous."

"What is happening to society?" Helen said, shaking her head in disgust. "So many sick people."

"Yes," Dustin replied, dialing Jeremy. "And it isn't getting any better. Places like the dark web don't help either."

Beth moved closer to Carissa. "Tell me the truth… do you think we'll get Lainey back?" she asked quietly.

It was the one thing Carissa never usually knew for sure, and trying to explain that she didn't know, yet still sound credible as a psychic, was often very challenging.

"I'm sorry. I want to believe you will; I just can't give you a solid answer," she said, reaching out to Beth. She touched her hand and was rewarded with some insight on Lainey's mother. Beth was a woman who loved her daughter more than anything, and the guilt of losing Lainey was eating her up inside. Carissa also felt something else that surprised her. She had some interesting doubts about Tom in regards to their missing child.

Noticing the curious look on Carissa's face when she pulled her hand back, Beth asked if something was wrong.

Carissa glanced at Tom. Obviously, she couldn't bring it up in front of him. She decided she'd try and speak to Beth alone later.

"Nothing is wrong. I just tapped into your emotions there for a second and felt your pain. I promise, we'll do whatever we can to get Lainey back," she replied softly.

Beth relaxed. "Thank you."

"GOOD NEWS. I spoke to Jeremy and he's agreed to check into a few things," Dustin said a short time later, putting his phone away. He looked at William. "I sent him a picture of Lainey and he's going to dive right in and see if he can come up with something for us."

"Excellent," said William, looking relieved. "We appreciate anything he can do."

"Just like Carissa, he'll try doing what he's best at, but again. No guarantees," Dustin said, looking around at everyone.

"We understand," said Beth.

"So, what else do you suggest we do?" Tom asked, folding his arms across his chest. "I don't know about everyone else, but I feel like we should be doing a lot more than this."

"I agree," said William.

"Obviously, you need to keep spreading the word, especially through the media. Hell, even letting them know that you're speaking with a psychic is something they might be interested in reporting," said Dustin.

"Yes. It's good to keep Lainey's name and face in the news," Carissa added.

Dustin looked at Carissa. "I also think it would be a good idea to have Carissa visit Lainey's room. She might be able to make a better connection."

Carissa nodded. "I was going to suggest that myself."

"Whatever you think will help," Beth said.

Carissa caught Tom rolling his eyes and knew right away that he believed her to be a fraud.

Time to fix that.

"Thank you so much for giving me this chance to help find your daughter," she said, walking over to him. She held out her

73

hand. "Like I mentioned earlier, I'll do whatever I can to bring her home to you."

Tom reached out and shook Carissa's hand. "We appreciate you trying to help," he replied.

Feelings of guilt and shame flooded Carissa's senses. Tom blamed himself for Lainey's disappearance, but she couldn't tell why exactly. She decided to focus on something else. Pointing out that he felt guilty about his daughter's disappearance was something anyone could pick up on. After all, he was a parent.

"Tom, your father died when you were a teenager. He had a… gambling addiction," Carissa said, seeing a vision of playing cards and money. She also sensed that his father had been an alcoholic and died of possibly liver disease or cancer.

Tom pulled his hand away. "Yeah," he replied, looking guarded. "Did Beth tell you that?"

"We've never spoken," Beth said, expecting his response. Getting more information, she went on. "Your mother and you are not on speaking terms. Although, it's mostly by your choice."

"She's upset about our divorce," Tom muttered. "Every time we talk, it turns into an argument."

"Yes. It's because she thinks you're following in your father's footprints. She's just frightened," Carissa told him.

Tom didn't say anything.

"Seriously, though. You should call her and let her know about Lainey," Carissa replied.

Beth's jaw dropped. "Tom, you didn't tell your mother yet?"

"We haven't spoken since you and I separated," he replied, unable to meet Beth's eyes. "Anyway, we should be talking about how to find Lainey. Not about my personal life."

"She needs to know," Beth said curtly. "And if you're not going to call her, I will."

Tom sighed. "Fine, Beth. I'll call her."

74

Dustin looked at his watch. "We should head back to your place, Beth, and see if Carissa can pick up anything. Who knows, maybe her kidnapper has visited your place in the past?"

Beth grunted. "It's so hard to believe that anyone we know could really be involved."

"You'd be surprised by what some people will do for money. Especially, if they're desperate enough," Dustin said.

Carissa noticed Beth's eyes dart to Tom and knew there definitely was a certain level of mistrust there.

Chapter 13

Lainey

DINA MADE LAINEY take a shower, and afterward, she was given a sleeveless white dress to put on for the photos. Once dressed, Tara helped dry her hair while she sat in front of a full-length mirror, watching.

"Sorry," Tara said, trying to comb through some of the snarls. "We ran out of conditioner."

Lainey didn't care about the conditioner or anything other than going home.

Tara's forehead creased when she asked about seeing her mother again.

"Kiddo, it's never going to happen. I'm sorry. You have to quit talking about it."

Lainey stared at Tara's reflection in the mirror. "Can't *you* bring me home?"

"I can't. I told you before, I'm just as much of a prisoner as you are," Tara mumbled.

Lainey knew she was able to move freely around the house. Surely, Tara could walk out the front door when nobody was looking? "Well, can't we *sneak* out? While they're all asleep?"

"I tried that once. They almost killed me, I was beaten so badly."

Lainey's eyes widened.

"Just… look, there's no way we can leave, and if we did, they'd catch us," she said bitterly.

"But what if they didn't? I can run really fast."

Tara's eyes softened. "I'm sure you can. But, Lainey, they have guns. You can't outrun a bullet."

Lainey's heart sank. Deep down, she'd been hoping Tara would help, especially after Yury said she had to make movies. Lainey didn't know what kind they were talking about, but figured they couldn't be good because she'd gotten pretty upset.

A loud pounding on the door made them both jump.

"You almost done?" Kurt asked, opening the bedroom door and peering inside.

"Yes," replied Tara, setting the comb down.

Kurt stepped into the room and smiled. "Hi there, princess," he said, holding his hand out to Lainey. "Let's see how you look."

Lainey was too terrified of the man to resist. She took his hand and stood up.

"Look at you. You *have* to be the prettiest girl I've ever seen," he said, nodding in satisfaction. He winked at Tara. "Aside from you, of course."

Tara rolled her eyes.

Kurt pointed to Lainey's mouth. "By the way, put some of that lip gloss on her."

"My mom doesn't let me wear makeup," Lainey said.

He smiled in amusement. "Believe me, kid, she isn't going to know about it." Kurt looked at Tara, who was glaring at him. "Is there a problem?"

"You swore that I wouldn't have to make films if I helped with the kids," Tara said angrily. "You promised me."

77

Sighing, Kurt pulled out a cigarette and lit the end of it. "I don't make the rules. Yury does."

Tara's eyes darted to Lainey and then back to Kurt. "When is he leaving?"

Kurt blew out a puff of smoke. "Sunday. He's taking you with him, it sounds like. Just like he mentioned downstairs."

"It's not fair," said Tara, tears springing to her eyes. "You promised me... I helped you with the kids.... You lied to me!"

Kurt put his arm around her shoulders. "Relax. If you cooperate with him, Yury will take good care of you."

She shrugged his arm away from her. "I don't care. I don't want to do this."

"You have no choice," Kurt replied, walking toward the door. He turned back. "Look, don't make it harder than it has to be. You're going no matter what, so don't give him any reason to hurt you."

Tara stared at him with resentment. "Maybe I'd rather die than do those films," she said in a hollow voice.

"Don't be so dramatic," he said.

Tara raised her chin. "I wasn't trying to be."

Sighing, Kurt nodded toward Lainey. "Bring her downstairs. I'm going to check on Sammy," he said, walking out the door.

Tara stood there motionless, staring off into space, as his footsteps receded.

Lainey cleared her throat. "What kind of movies is he talking about?"

Wiping the tears from her eyes, she walked over and grabbed a tissue from the nightstand. "Bad ones. Pornos."

"What are those?"

"Sex films," Tara replied miserably. "Let's go."

Shocked, Lainey followed Tara out of the bedroom. "You're going to be in those?" she whispered.

78

Tara laughed coldly. "Not if I can help it."

Lainey wondered what she meant about not doing them, but didn't ask. She was almost too afraid to. Tara was clearly upset and in no mood to talk about it.

The two girls headed down the staircase. As they moved through the foyer, Tara stopped and stared at the front door.

"Tara?" whispered Lainey. Her heart began to pound. *Was she thinking about leaving?*

Before Tara could answer, the staircase creaked.

Both girls looked up to find Dina and Sammy descending the steps toward them. Like Lainey, he wore white, but with a black tie and pants. It was obvious he'd also had a shower as his curly blond hair was combed over to the side and still damp.

Kurt walked out into the foyer. "Everybody ready?"

"Yeah," replied Tara, not looking at him.

"Then let's get a move-on," he said.

They stepped into the parlor, where Yury was setting up a backdrop for the photos.

Kurt walked over to the buffet. "I need something stiffer than a beer. A whiskey-seven sounds good. I'll be happy to mix you up one, Dina. I know you like 'em."

"Yes. Thank you," she said, letting go of Sammy's hand.

"Tara?" he asked, looking back over his shoulder. "Something to take the edge off?"

Tara rolled her eyes.

"You're still pissed off?" Kurt asked, filling a small glass with ice.

She didn't respond.

He let out a ragged sigh. "I guess that answers that. Lainey? Sammy? Would you like something to drink?"

"No. They're both fine," Tara said firmly before Lainey could answer.

79

"What's with the attitude?" Yury asked, turning around.

"She's upset about doing films," Kurt explained.

"I don't know why. There are worse things one could be doing," Yury, said, fiddling with his camera. "Besides, I'm a generous man. You do well, we both make money, and who knows? You might one day get your own apartment."

Tara sat down on the sofa. "Yaay. Thrilling," she muttered.

"She's a stubborn one, I give her that," Yury said to Kurt, smiling in amusement. "But, we can work with that."

Kurt sighed and looked at Sammy. "Kiddo, you want something to drink?"

"Leave them alone," Tara said in a cold voice. "Why can't you just take the photos and let them go back to their rooms?"

"Enough," said Yury angrily, looking back at her again, his eyes hard. "I'm getting tired of your mouth. You shut it or I will."

Tara's face paled. She looked down at her hands.

"Teenagers, huh?" laughed Kurt nervously. "You want a drink, Yury?"

"Yes. I will take a vodka-sour," Yury said. "Something tells me I'm going to need it tonight."

Chapter 14

Carissa

WHEN CARISSA STEPPED into Beth's home, she was met with different variables of somatic energy. Fear. Sadness. Anger. Hopelessness. Guilt. Everything one would expect during such a terrible time. She also became conscious of something else that was of great importance.

She quickly pulled Dustin aside. "I'm fairly certain that someone who has actually stepped foot in here took Lainey," she whispered excitedly.

His eyes widened. "You're serious?"

She nodded.

"Do you think it's Tom?" he asked, glancing toward Lainey's father, who was on his cell phone.

She'd already voiced her concerns about Tom on the ride over. Not only was he hiding something, which even she couldn't quite grasp, he might certainly have a valid motive. Especially, if he was a serious gambler. The thought of him selling his daughter, however, seemed over the top. As much as it was always possible, she sensed that Tom's love for his daughter, as well as his ex, would never allow him to stoop so low. At least, she hoped.

"I have a hard time believing he'd do it," she whispered.

"But you're not certain?"

Carissa looked over at Tom again. There'd only been a few times when she'd been 'certain' about someone's innocence. Unfortunately, this wasn't one of them. "No."

Beth hung up her jacket and walked over to them. "Have you picked up on something already?"

"I may have. Can I talk to you alone?" Carissa asked, unbuttoning her wool jacket.

"Yes. Of course," she replied. "Why don't you let me hang up your jacket and then we can go upstairs and talk in Lainey's room?"

'Sounds good." Carissa took it off and handed it to her. "You have a lovely home, by the way."

Beth smiled sadly. "It seems dull and empty to me now without my daughter home. But, thank you."

Carissa gave her a sympathetic smile. "She definitely gives this place life. I also feel it's hollow without her."

"It won't be the same unless we get her back," she replied in a husky voice.

Carissa nodded.

Choked up, Beth turned away and went to go hang up her jacket.

Helen, who'd disappeared into the kitchen, walked back into the living room. "I'm making some tea. Would anyone else like any? Or coffee? Or, hell, a shot of whiskey?"

William chuckled. "Does that go for me, too?"

She gave him a stern look. "You wish. Not with your high blood pressure. You can have some decaffeinated tea."

"Why does staying healthy have to be so boring?" William drawled, walking to the large picture window facing the street, where two news vans had just pulled up. He sighed. "Looks like the media is back."

"They must have gotten wind about Carissa helping us," Beth said, walking over to stand next to him.

82

"Great. I can see the headlines now," said Tom dryly. *"Desperate couple seek advice of psychic to find missing child.* My co-workers will never let me hear the end of this one."

"Why does it matter?" Beth said sharply. "I mean, if they give you crap about using every resource we can to find Lainey, then they can go screw themselves."

"I agree," said William, looking over his shoulder at Tom. "And if she helps locate my granddaughter, they'll be eating crow later."

Tom was silent.

"This is definitely good for us," Dustin said, walking up to the window. "The more coverage on Lainey, no matter what it's about, can only help."

As they watched the reporters and camera crew unload out of the news trucks, Carissa followed Beth upstairs to Lainey's room.

"Cute," Carissa said when she walked inside. The furniture was white, including the small desk in the corner. The walls were light blue and decorated with posters of kittens and puppies.

"We just painted it recently. It was pink and now Lainey wants nothing to do with the color."

"She's outgrown it, huh?" Carissa asked, amused.

"Yes. It's too girly, apparently."

Carissa smiled and looked at the posters. "She wants a pet, doesn't she?"

"Yes. She's been begging for a dog." Beth shut the door and sat down on the blue and green bedspread. "Mike, my fiancé, is allergic to them though. So, it's probably not going to happen."

"What about a cat?"

"Mike doesn't like them," she replied. "Unfortunately."

Carissa closed her eyes for a minute and took a deep breath. After a few seconds, she looked at Beth again. "I feel as if… Lainey thought you and Tom were going to get back together. She's not very happy about you and Mike getting married, is she?"

"No. It's going to take some time, but," she smiled wanly, "she'll get over it."

Carissa looked over at Lainey's dresser and suddenly had a vision of socks.

"Does Lainey have a big sock collection?" she asked.

"No," said Beth, looking amused. "Why?"

"I don't know. I just keep seeing socks. It's strange."

Carissa brushed it off and continued looking around the room, trying to get a better understanding of what kind of girl Lainey was. Intuition told her that she spent a lot of time alone. Drawing pictures and playing computer games. Too much time in her bedroom, for someone so young. "Your daughter is very shy and has a hard time making friends, doesn't she?"

Beth looked surprised. "Yes. She does have a couple at school, but is so shy that she often feels left out of things."

"The other kids don't always see her," Carissa replied.

She frowned. "What do you mean? I don't understand."

"Lainey hangs back from the crowd and is afraid of being rejected. So instead of taking a chance, and being hurt, she won't make the first move in developing a friendship with someone new."

"Yes, that definitely sounds like her," Beth replied with a sad smile. "When Tom and I separated, I noticed she became less outgoing in general."

"It's an insecurity thing, but I really feel as if she'll get over it," Carissa said. "You know, sometimes children blame themselves for their parents' separation."

"I heard that, too. Which is why I sat down with her and we talked about the divorce and how she was definitely not to blame,"

Beth said, sounding surprised. "I mean, I didn't tell her about Tom's gambling. I just told her that we'd grown apart."

"I'm sure as she gets older, she'll have a better understanding. You could always tell her the truth. That he'd developed some habits that you didn't care for."

"Maybe. Tom said he quit gambling, however." She smiled wryly. "I could see Lainey trying to get us back together if she thought it was the only reason we broke up in the first place."

"But wasn't it the main reason?"

"Yes, but we also fought a lot."

"Because of the gambling," said Carissa.

Beth sighed. "Yes. Still, it's too late. We've both moved on."

Carissa wanted to tell her that Tom hadn't, but she wasn't there to bring the couple back together.

"Speaking of Lainey having friends, you mentioned there are a couple she's really close with, right?"

"Yes."

"Have their parents been in the house lately?" Carissa asked.

"No. Not for a long time, actually."

Something niggled in the back of her mind about Beth's fiancé. She felt like she needed to ask more questions about him. "What does Mike to for a living?"

"He owns an art gallery in Minneapolis."

"Ah. He doesn't live here with you, does he?"

"No. In fact, Lainey and I will be moving into his place after the wedding." Beth's eyes suddenly filled with tears. She picked up a small, stuffed llama from the bed and stared down at it sadly. "We're supposed to, at least."

"Where is Mike at the moment?"

"Out of town on a business trip. Madison."

"Does he often travel a lot?" she asked. With her daughter being gone, it seemed a little strange that Mike wasn't around to show his support.

"Only when he and Mitch are going to be holding a show and need to find art to fill it."

"Mike is an artist, then?" said Carissa, imagining him with a paintbrush. Her intuition told her that Mike was very passionate about his work and spent grueling hours locked away in his studio.

"Yes. A very good one. I'll have to show you the painting he just made recently. It's of Lainey and me. He's incredible."

Carissa smiled. "I would love to see it."

"It's downstairs. I haven't hung it up yet. We're moving into his place soon and I figured I'd wait until then."

Carissa imagined that she'd also not put it up because she knew it would upset Tom.

"How does Tom feel about your engagement?"

"We don't really talk about it. It's really none of his business and I know it probably bothers him anyway."

"I'm sure," Carissa replied, trying to tune into Tom again. From what she gathered, he was feeling a lot of guilt about why they split up. She shared that with Beth.

"At least he isn't blaming it on me," she replied, wiping her tears.

"He knows it was him and… nobody could blame you for not wanting that kind of stress in your life," she told her. Carissa sensed there were times when Beth wondered if she'd made the right choice and even felt a bit regretful. "Speaking of his gambling, did he ever owe any large sums of money?"

"Not that I'm aware of. I mean, he spent too much when we were together, but I don't think he ever ran up any big gambling debts."

86

They talked some more about Tom, and Beth asked her point-blank if Carissa thought he was involved.

She pictured the brooding man in her head. "I don't think so."

Beth relaxed and sighed in relief. "I was worried there for a second that you were going to tell me otherwise."

Carissa gave her a sympathetic smile. "You still have some feelings for him."

"I suppose part of me always will love him." She stared off into space. "I try not to think about what could have been if he'd given it up because it's painful. Other than the gambling, he was the perfect husband and father."

Carissa nodded.

"I know I already asked, but… do you think we'll find her?" Beth asked.

Carissa wanted to console Beth and tell her not to worry. Tell her that Lainey would be found and everything would be okay, like most might in similar situation. But, she didn't dare. She'd learned that as a psychic, it wasn't wise to give any kind of false hope, as it could be held against her later.

"I am hopeful we will, but I can't always see the outcome of situations like this. Dustin and I will both do whatever we can to try and locate her."

"I understand," she replied softly. "By the way, did you see the news about the missing boy?"

"No, but Dustin told me about it."

"Do you think the same people might have taken him?"

Carissa let out a sigh. "I don't really know. It's always possible, I guess. I've been so focused on Lainey that I haven't given it much thought."

Beth sighed. "I feel like I should reach out to Sammy's parents."

"You could. In fact, I might want to do that myself to see if I feel any connection."

"I'll see if I can arrange something," Beth said.

"There is one thing I wanted to share with you that's a little disturbing. I feel that someone, who has been in your house, is responsible for taking Lainey," Carissa confided. "Do you have many visitors or has anyone been here recently doing repairs?

"Wait a second," Beth said, her eyes wide. "I had someone here, about a month ago, replacing my water heater. He was an older guy in his fifties. Very friendly. I think his name was Bernie."

"Did he come in contact with Lainey?" Carissa asked.

"Yes. He was here for at least an hour and she was definitely home. It was on a Saturday." Beth looked stricken. "He made a comment about her. Said that she was lovely, in fact. Do you think he might have taken her?"

Carissa stood up. She wasn't getting any vibes about the man at all, but also hadn't met him. "I don't know, but we can't rule him out. You didn't tell the police about him?"

"To be honest, I totally forgot all about the guy." She groaned. "I feel like such an idiot for not thinking about him. He seemed so nice, but I guess that doesn't make him innocent."

"Being nice doesn't make him guilty, either, but he should definitely be checked out. Let's go and talk to Dustin. "

Chapter 15

Tara

TARA WATCHED YURY take pictures of Lainey and Sammy for the auction, her stomach twisting with fear and loathing. Although they'd left clothes on the children, Tara knew what awaited them would be more horrifying than posing in the nude. They would be sold and delivered to rich perverts who would do unspeakable things to them. Some of which Tara had undergone herself by the hands of Kurt, the sick, twisted asshole.

She glanced over at him as he paced in and out of the parlor, talking on his cell phone. She hated him so much, and yet, she knew that Kurt was all she had for protection against Yury and the rest of the people involved in their organization. Yes, he'd done some terrible things to her, but she didn't fear for her life. Not like she did around Yury, although there were times when she would have gladly welcomed death. The only thing that had kept her half sane was that ever since she'd grown a more womanly figure, Kurt had stopped touching her.

"Maybe I should get some pictures of you, too," Yury said, now looking over at Tara. "For your…" he smirked, "*modeling* portfolio."

She looked away, pretending she didn't hear him.

"Tara," snapped Yury. "Look at me when I speak to you."

89

Swallowing the lump in her throat, she turned to face him.

"Now," he twirled his finger around. "Undress."

"Please. No," she begged, panicking. "Don't make me do this."

"You wish some privacy?" Yury looked at Dina and instructed her to take the children back up to their rooms.

"Come," Dina said, grabbing both Lainey's and Sammy's hands.

Tara began to plead and beg again. The very idea of stripping in front of Yury made her sick to her stomach.

Kurt, stepping back into the parlor, noticed their exchange. "What's going on?" he asked, ending the call.

"We're going to take some pictures of Tara," Yury said, leering at her. "Hey. Did you not hear me? Remove your clothing."

Shaking her head, Tara backed away.

The big man balled up his fists and began moving toward her. "So, you want to do this the hard way, huh?"

Kurt moved between them. "There's no time for this. We need to meet with Hawk. He insists on seeing you."

Yury's thick eyebrows rose. "Me? Why?"

"He wants the rest of his money for the last two kids," said Kurt.

"He'll get paid after the auction," Yury replied, looking irritated. "Like always. He should know this by now."

"Apparently, he needs the money now and can't wait."

Yury grunted. "Tough shit. That's not how we do things."

"I tried telling him that, but he wouldn't listen. I have a feeling that something is going on. Normally he isn't impatient like this."

"What do you mean, you think something is going on?" Yury asked, scowling.

"I don't know exactly, but… he's acting strange. We need to find out why," Kurt said, looking troubled.

90

Yury let out a frustrated sigh. "Fine. We will talk. Is he on his way?"

"No, he said he'd meet us at Ned's Bar. It's only a couple of miles south of here."

"This guy of yours is really pissing me off. You know this doesn't make me happy," growled Yury.

"Yeah, it's kind of pissing me off, too. But, something is obviously going on and I'd like to get to the bottom of it."

"I'll get whatever it is out of him." Yury looked over at Tara. "And you. When we get back, we'll finish this discussion."

She looked away.

"Make sure Dina keeps an eye on her while we're gone," Yury told Kurt. "I don't trust her."

He nodded.

"I'm going to use the bathroom," Yury said, finishing his drink. "Then we head out."

When Yury left the parlor, Tara begged Kurt not to let him take pictures of her.

"Don't worry about him," Kurt said, trying to calm her. "We won't be back until late and I'm sure he'll have forgotten about it."

Tara knew Kurt. His words meant nothing and were just meant to placate her. They both knew that once Yury put his mind on something, he wouldn't let it go.

Dina stepped back into the room. "Kids put away."

"Good." Kurt grabbed his jacket from the chair he'd set it on earlier. "There's an emergency. Yury and I are leaving for a couple of hours. Lock everyone inside until we return."

Dina's eyes widened. "Tara, too?"

Nodding, he avoided eye-contact with Tara.

Seeing Dina's smug smile, Tara clenched her teeth and stormed out of the parlor. It was hard to conceive that the woman could be so cold and bitchy, especially since she'd also been abducted by

91

Yury as a child. But, Dina had somehow gained his trust over the years and was now both a gatekeeper and caretaker. Not only did they pay her well, but she could come and go whenever she wanted.

As Tara passed by Lainey's bedroom, she could hear the girl crying inside. Hesitating outside of the door, she wished she could do more. But Tara was too frightened to even consider it. The last time she'd tried running, she'd ended up with a few broken bones and the kind of pain she never wanted to feel again.

Dina tapped her on the shoulder. "Get to your room."

Before she could answer, Tara overheard Yury and Kurt arguing down below in the foyer.

"I don't care. Dina can take care of the kids. Tara will do movies and earn her keep. I will teach her how to please a man. Maybe I will even start tonight," he said with a smile in his voice."

Tara began to panic.

Yury was going to rape me.

She looked at Dina, hoping that for once, the other woman might show some kind of empathy. Instead, she saw nothing in her expression that indicated she even had a soul.

"Sounds like busy night for you," Dina said with a glint in her eyes as the two men left the house.

A sudden impulse to knock Dina flat on her ass and run like hell swept through her.

Dina's eyes narrowed. "Tara. No funny business," she mumbled, as if reading her mind.

Gritting her teeth, Tara stormed away from Lainey's room and stepped inside her own. As she stared at the bed, she thought about Yury's words and knew she'd rather die than let the pig put his hands on her.

I have to get out of here. If I don't make it, at least I'll be too badly beaten for him to rape me.

92

At least, she hoped…

"Wait, Dina," Tara called out as she heard the key in the door handle. "I'm thirsty. Can you get me something to drink?"

"You have water in bathroom," the woman said in her choppy English.

"It's well water. It tastes horrible. Can you get me something from the refrigerator? I promise not to make any trouble for you if you'll do me this one favor," she lied.

Dina huffed. "Fine."

Tara imagined Dina spitting into the beverage. It certainly wouldn't surprise her.

Tara looked around the bedroom for a weapon to use. Not seeing anything but a thin, metal lamp, she removed the dusty shade and unplugged it. Darkness settled upon the room. With her heart hammering in her chest, she stepped over to the bedroom door and waited for Dina to return. It was time to try and take back her life.

Chapter 16

Carissa

CARISSA AND BETH walked into the living room, where the others were watching the news.

"They still haven't found that little boy, Sammy Johnson, yet," Helen said sadly.

"That's too bad," Carissa said, looking at the television. They showed a photo of the boy, who also had blond hair and blue eyes. He was a little older than Lainey, and a good-looking kid.

"I've thought of something," Beth said, staring at the television, a sad expression on her face.

"What is it?" Dustin asked.

She told him about the repairman. "It might not mean anything, but… I think it's something worth checking out," Beth said.

Tom turned off the television and stood up. "Call Detective Samuels and let him know," he said, excited.

She walked to her purse and pulled out her cell phone.

"What do you think, Carissa?" Dustin asked. "About this repairman?"

"Honestly, I'm not clear about him," she admitted, sitting down on the sofa. Rubbing her forehead, Carissa let out a frustrated sigh. "I feel we're so close to finding out who the kidnapper is, and yet, he also seems so far out of reach. It's frustrating."

"You think we're really that close?" William asked.

She nodded. "Definitely. It's like when you're trying to remember the name of an actor and it's at the tip of your tongue, but you just can't think of it? That's how I'm feeling right now."

Dustin walked over and put a comforting hand on her shoulder. "Don't be so hard on yourself."

"Wait a second, do you really believe that someone close to us has kidnapped my daughter?" Tom asked, looking confused and angry.

"Yes," she said. "Or someone who's recently been in contact with her."

"Detective Samuels didn't answer, but I left him a message," Beth said, putting her phone away.

"Did you get a receipt from this Bernie guy or get his card?" Dustin asked.

"Yes," she said, her face brightening. "It's in the kitchen." Beth disappeared and returned shortly with both. She gave Dustin the paperwork. "See. His name is Bernie Smith."

Dustin looked over the receipt. "I've heard of this place. It's a small repair shop in Roseville. Bernie might even be the owner."

"I don't think he is," Beth said. "He mentioned something about his boss waking up on the wrong side of the bed that morning and being grumpy."

"He was talking about his wife," Carissa said, the knowledge making her smile. "At least, I think."

Dustin pulled out his cell phone. "Let me call Jeremy back and see if he can run some background checks on this guy. He might have a record, you never know."

"Maybe he'll have found some information for us by now, too," Carissa reminded him.

"That would certainly be nice," Dustin replied, putting the phone up to his ear.

IT TURNED OUT that Jeremy wasn't having much luck searching for information on the dark web. Not yet, anyway. He agreed to check on Bernie Smith and told Dustin to stop by later.

"He's going to keep looking, though, right?" William asked, after Dustin hung up.

"Definitely," he said and looked at Carissa. "In the meantime, I think you and I should swing by this repair shop. Maybe we'll run into Bernie and you can feel him out."

"It's already after six. They might not be open," she replied, looking at her cell phone.

"The hours are nine-to-seven," Dustin replied, checking the receipt. "If we leave now, we'll get there before they close."

She grabbed her purse. "Okay."

Tom, who'd been sitting on the sofa, stood up. "I'd like to go with you."

Carissa knew it was a bad idea. He would take one look at Bernie and start jumping to conclusions. Desperate to find Lainey, everyone looked guilty at the moment.

"You should stay here with Beth," Carissa told him. "And wait for the cops to call back."

Tom started to argue.

"It's a bad idea," Carissa said firmly. "And the only reason we're going is to see if I feel any bad vibes about this man. If you're in the room with us, I'll only feel your anger and that's not going to help Lainey."

"She's right," Beth said. "We need to let Carissa do what she does best. I'm sure if she thinks he has anything to do with it, she'll call us right away."

"I will," Carissa promised.

Tom let out a frustrated sigh. "Fine."

Chapter 17

Tara

TARA WAITED IN the darkness, listening for Dina's foot-steps. After about five minutes, she heard the click of the woman's heels as she approached the bedroom. Holding her breath, Tara waited.

Dina opened up the door and stepped inside. "Oh, no," she said, flipping the light-switch on and off.

Heart pounding, Tara stepped around the door and swung the lamp, hitting Dina on the side of the head so hard, it knocked her out. The woman collapsed to the floor, dropping the uncapped bottle of water, its contents spilling everywhere.

Although she despised Dina, Tara's eyes filled with tears. "I'm sorry," she mumbled, dropping the lamp.

Dina obviously didn't respond.

Trembling, Tara leaned down and checked her pulse. Relieved that she had one, she grabbed Dina's ring of keys, and raced down the hallway to Lainey's room. Her hands shook as she unlocked the door.

Lainey stared at her groggily from the bed as she flipped on the light-switch. "Tara? What's going on?"

She hurried over to the bed and held out her hand. "Come on. We're getting out of here."

Lainey gasped, threw back the covers, and scrambled out of bed. "Really?"

"Yes. Really," she said. "We have to hurry, though."

Lainey looked down at the pajamas she'd been given. "Should I change into something else?"

"No time. Just, keep that on," Tara said, rushing over to the old, knotty pine dresser. Dina had recently purchased a bunch of new clothing, in all different sizes, from the Goodwill, but the pajamas would do. "I'll find you some socks. Wait a second," she said looking around. "Where are your shoes?"

"I don't know," Lainey said. "I haven't seen them for a while."

Tara pulled open one of the drawers and grabbed two pairs of socks. "Hopefully, they're downstairs in the closet. Put both pairs on though. Just in case."

Lainey started pulling the first sock over her foot, but was moving so slowly that it made Tara nervous. Half expecting Dina to walk in on them at any minute, she lost her patience.

"Here, let me help," she said, grabbing the socks from her. She quickly pulled both pairs over Lainey's feet and then helped her up. "We have to get Sammy, too."

"What about Dina and the men?" Lainey asked, following her to the door.

"They left," she said, peeking out the door. Not seeing Dina, she motioned for Lainey to follow. The two rushed over to Sammy's room and Tara unlocked the door.

"Sammy," she said, flipping on the lights. "Get up."

The little boy stared at them in confusion, his eyelids heavy. "What's going on?"

"We're leaving," Lainey said.

His eyes widened. "We are?"

"Yes. Come on. We have to move quickly," Tara said, rushing over to the dresser.

99

Sammy climbed out of bed and Tara helped him put socks on his feet as well. Afterward, they stood up and she looked around. "Your shoes are missing, too, huh?" she mumbled, scowling. "Dang it."

"I haven't seen them," he replied with a shrug.

"Hopefully, they're downstairs by the doorway. Let's go," Tara said.

The three raced out of the bedroom and headed down the steps.

"Are there any more kids here?" Lainey whispered, looking back over her shoulder toward the top of the staircase.

"Not right now," Tara replied staring at the doorway ahead, expecting Yury or Kurt to walk in while they were trying to escape.

"Where is everyone?" Sammy asked softly.

Before she could answer, a noise at the top of the steps made them all look back.

It was Dina.

"You're dead," she snapped, staring at Tara with murder in her eyes and blood dripping down the side of her face.

The kids gasped.

Dina raced down toward them.

Panicking, Tara rushed to the front door and tried opening it. It was locked.

Before she could attempt to use one of the keys to try and open it, Dina pounced on her.

Lainey stared in horror as Dina grabbed Tara by the neck and began choking her. "No!" she screamed.

The teenager dropped the keys and dug her fingernails into Dina's hands, trying to get her to release her grip.

Crying out in pain, the older woman let go of her neck.

"You bitch!" gasped Tara. She balled up her fist and hit Dina in the face, knocking her backward.

100

Stumbling, the woman lost her balance and collapsed at the bottom of the steps. Blood began to gush out of her nose and she let out an angry howl.

Picking up the keys, Tara rushed to the doorway. With one eye on Dina and the other on the keys, she somehow managed to unlock the door.

"You're stupid," Dina said, rising slowly to her feet while holding her bloody nose. "They'll find you."

Ignoring her, Tara opened the door. "Come on," she said to the children, wishing there was time to look for their shoes. But she knew Dina had probably sent Kurt and Yury a message already. More than likely, they were already on their way back to the farmhouse.

Sammy rushed outside, followed by Lainey. Soon all three of them were racing away from the porch and into the cold, dark November night.

Chapter 18

Carissa

"I HATE THESE short days," Dustin said, referring to the fact that it was already dark outside. "And this damn snow. It's only November. I must have missed autumn when I blinked."

Carissa grinned. "I know. Fall never lasts long enough for me." She looked up at the sky. It was snowing—big, soft fluffy flakes. Although it was pretty, she could definitely do without more of it. Especially after the blizzard she'd experienced in Two Harbors the week before. "I like the darkness, though. I'm a night owl, you know me," Carissa replied as they pulled away from Beth's house.

Amused, Dustin's eyes danced. "That's right. Darkness and spooky things have always fascinated you."

She grinned. "The supernatural is what fascinates me."

"Wish I could say the same. It creeps the hell out of me."

"Including me?" she teased.

"Yeah, you definitely do. But that's because you're a woman. You people are terrifying."

Carissa laughed.

He stared at her affectionately. "I miss that. Your laughter."

She didn't reply, although she felt the same way about him. Not only his laughter she missed, but his corny jokes. Then there was his cooking, which was so much better than hers. His ability to remember small details, including her favorite brand and color of lipstick and least favorite vegetable. And the way he was around children. For someone who'd never had any, it was obvious he adored kids. Which was another reason why Dustin chose the cases he did. He needed to save or avenge the innocent.

They drove in silence for a while, listening to the radio. When a commercial came on, he turned down the volume and asked her about Tom. "So, you really don't think he's involved?"

"No. I don't know if this repairman is either." She leaned back and sighed. "I just needed to get out of the house. There were so many emotions swirling around in there, it was clouding my mind."

He nodded. "I understand. You know, there's one person we haven't met yet. Beth's fiancé. I don't know about you, but I'm kind of curious about him. Did Beth say much?"

"Only that he paints and is also an art dealer. I think she mentioned that he'll be back in town late tonight. We could stop by tomorrow and talk to him."

"Yeah." He sighed. "I'm hoping someone will have found Lainey by then, though."

She nodded. "I know. I hope so, too. Still, I just can't believe Mike is out traveling when Beth needs his support. Talk about insensitive."

"We shouldn't jump to conclusions. He might not have been able to get out of it," Dustin replied. "It's not like he's traveling for fun."

He was right.

When had she gotten so cynical of people?

"True," she said as they approached a stoplight.

"You don't think he's involved, do you?" he asked, looking at her curiously as they waited for the light to turn green.

"I don't know. I'd have to meet him, I guess, to know for sure."

"Beth mentioned that he has a son. I can't imagine a family man being involved. Especially one she's engaged to."

"I know."

"Still, you're pretty confident that the kidnapper stepped inside of Beth's home?"

"Yes." An image of an airplane suddenly flashed through her mind. "I'm also pretty confident that if we don't figure something out soon, Lainey will be lost to us forever," she said, imagining the child being forced onto it.

Dustin sighed. "Me, too."

WHEN THEY ARRIVED at the repair shop, there were two employees inside. One a middle-aged guy with glasses, the other, a man who looked to be in his thirties. Carissa guessed them to be father and son.

"Can I help you?" asked the older man, standing at the register. He wore a light-blue polo shirt with the company logo and the name Bernie inscribed on the front. He had a stack of invoices in front of him and appeared to be going through them.

"We're in the market for a new water-heater," Dustin lied. "I know you're almost closing for the night, so we'll just take a quick look around and then get out of your hair."

"Hey, don't worry about it. My son, Dan, here will show you where they are and help answer any questions you might have," Bernie said with a friendly smile.

"Yes, definitely," Dan said.

"Thanks," Dustin replied.

As they followed Dan over to the water-heaters, Carissa tried getting a read on Bernie. She couldn't come up with much, especially since he was so absorbed in what he was doing. She looked at the clock and knew there wasn't much time to waste. She needed to get closer to him.

"I'll be right back," she said to Dustin and Dan, who were already talking appliances.

Dustin nodded.

Carissa strolled back over to Bernie. "You know, you look really familiar," she said, tapping her chin.

He looked up from his paperwork. "Oh?"

"Yeah. I just can't place it."

"Maybe you've seen me on television?" he asked, looking amused. "We had a commercial at the end of the summer."

She reached out and touched his hand. "You know what? That just might be it. I usually never forget a face."

"Especially an ugly mug like mine," he joked, a twinkle in his eyes.

"Nonsense. You're not ugly and your wife would slap you silly if she heard you talking like that," she chided, removing her hand. "Her name is Wanda, isn't it?"

He stared at her in surprise. "Why yes. Yes it is. How did you know?"

She smiled. There wasn't anything creepy or evil about Bernie, as far as she could tell. The man was happily married and had a life filled with grandchildren and Golden Retrievers. She sensed he'd rather get run over by a train than hurt a child. "Lucky guess?"

"Very lucky," he said, removing his eyeglasses. Staring at her, he began cleaning the lenses. "You know, you actually look familiar to me. I think I may have seen your picture somewhere recently."

She pictured him reading the papers and knew what he was going to say before the words left his lips.

Bernie's eyes widened in recognition. "Wait a second. You helped solve that case about the missing girl up in Two Harbors last weekend. That *was* you, wasn't it?"

Carissa grinned. "You have a great memory."

He chuckled. "My wife would beg to differ. Anyway, our granddaughter, Misty, attends college up in Duluth. She told us about the case first and then we read about it in the papers. We were all fascinated by your help in finding the little girl. Great job, by the way."

"Thank you."

"Dan," called Bernie. "This here is that psychic Misty told us about. The one who found that missing child up north."

His son looked just as surprised. "Really?"

"Could I get a picture of you to send to my granddaughter? She's going to freak out when she finds out you were here. Oh, and would it be too much trouble to get your autograph?"

Carissa blushed, not used to being treated like a celebrity. It was both flattering and a tiny bit awkward at the same time. "I... um... okay. If you really want it."

"Oh, she'll be thrilled." He pulled out his phone and snapped a couple of pictures. Afterward, he asked her to sign a business card.

"Thank you." He looked at the card she'd signed. "So, Ms. Jones, does my future look like I'll be getting some brownie points for this? If not, from my granddaughter, but from my lovely wife, Jane?"

She smiled. "If you really want brownie points, don't forget that her birthday is coming up soon."

Bernie gave her a stunned look. "It's tomorrow. Young lady, I think you just may have saved my marriage," he joked, breaking into a smile. "I've been so caught up in my inventory the past few days, it just slipped my mind."

Something told her it wouldn't have been the first time. Bernie was a nice man, but a little scatterbrained when it came to dates.

She leaned forward. "Take her out for Italian. It's her favorite, isn't it?"

He chuckled. "You have any ideas for a gift?"

"Sorry. You're on your own there," Carissa replied with a smile. Somehow, she suspected that Jane would consider the fact that he'd remembered her birthday as the best gift of all this year.

"SO, WHAT DID you think?" Dustin asked as they left the store.

"Definitely not involved."

Sighing, Dustin unlocked the truck. "I was afraid you were going to say that."

Chapter 19

Lainey

LAINEY'S FEET WERE chilled to the bone as she tried keeping up with Tara and Sammy along the narrow, dirt road. The socks provided little protection against the gravel and cold, and with every step, it became more and more difficult to run.

"Wait!" she gasped, having to stop to catch her breath. They weren't even that far from the house, maybe seven hundred yards, but Lainey was exhausted and her feet ached.

"Are you okay?" Tara asked, looking concerned.

"I'm cold and tired," Lainey replied, her teeth chattering.

"I know," Tara replied softly. She leaned down and touched Lainey's left foot. "I'm so sorry about this. I'd give you my shoes but you'd fall right out of them."

"Mine are cold, too, but it's better to be out here than inside with them," Sammy said, shifting from one foot to the other.

Tara looked back toward the farmhouse and then to where they were headed. "We need to get moving again. Before someone comes for us."

"Yeah, Lainey. I know you're cold but you'll be home soon. Think about that," Sammy said.

"Okay," she replied.

"Come on," Sammy said, grabbing her hand. "I'll help you."

"Thanks," Lainey replied.

They began moving again, this time at a slower pace. Unfortunately, it was starting to snow, making it more slippery for the children. If that wasn't bad enough, after another two-hundred yards, they saw headlights approaching in the distance.

Swearing, Tara stopped and turned toward the younger children. "Hurry! Run to the woods!"

"Come on, Lainey," Sammy said, pulling her with him.

The trio crossed over to the other side of the dirt road and headed toward the trees. Once they were deep enough in the woods, they crouched down and waited for the headlights to pass. It took a while for the car to move down the road, the occupants inside obviously searching for them.

"Is that them?" asked Sammy.

"Yes. It's Kurt's car," replied Tara.

They waited until the car reached the farmhouse and then took off again, back toward the road.

"Wait, what if they see us?" Lainey asked, stopping suddenly.

"It's too dark," Tara told her. "They'll only be able to see us if their headlights are shining our way."

"Oh. Good," she replied.

The three continued moving, fear and adrenaline driving them onward. Even Lainey, who couldn't feel her feet anymore, fought through the painful side-ache she was starting to have, and the rough, cold terrain. All she kept thinking about was her family. Her home. Her warm bed.

"You guys are doing great," Tara said, slowing down to catch her breath. "I can't believe we've gotten this far already."

"We're going to make it, aren't we?" Sammy said, a hopeful look on his face.

109

Tara glanced back. She could see the taillights of Kurt's car parked outside of the farmhouse.

She looked at the kids. "Yes. Just keep going. I'm sure there has to be a house coming up. We'll ask the people who live there for help. They can call the police for us."

"Okay," they replied.

Soon, they rounded a bend and the farmhouse was well out of sight. The trees began to taper off, and eventually, they reached a fork in the road.

"Which way do we go?" Sammy asked.

Tara sighed. She knew if they continued to go straight, they'd make it to the frontage road and then to the highway. But it was still a long way away, and with their luck, Kurt and Yury would find them. Especially since they'd be out in the open.

"This way," she said, deciding to go right. There were more trees ahead, and she might have been mistaken, but it looked like there were lights beyond.

Chapter 20

Carissa

HUNGRY, THEY WENT through a Taco Bell drive-through and decided to eat in his truck. Dustin requested extra packets of the spiciest salsa they carried, which amused Carissa.

"You have an iron stomach," she said as they pulled into one of the parking spots to eat.

He grinned. "Spicy food is good for you."

"Maybe for you. I get heartburn with the mildest of salsa."

"Don't be too hard on yourself. It does take a special kind of training to eat the way I do," he said, opening up the bag. "And a nearby restroom."

Carissa chuckled. "What's the joy in punishing yourself like that with such spicy food?"

"It tastes good." He gave her a half-smile. "I think."

Still smiling herself, she shook her head.

"So, Carissa, how's life been treating you?" Dustin asked softly as he opened up a packet of salsa and squirted some on his taco.

"Fine," she replied, knowing what he was really asking. "Busy. You?"

He licked his finger and threw the packet away. "Same. As much as I can, anyway. It's all I have right now. Without you."

111

She saw the pain in his eyes and looked away. "Dustin, you know this isn't a good time to talk about this. We have to stay focused on Lainey."

He finished chewing the bite he'd taken. "I know, but really, when is?" he replied, an edge to his voice. "The only time we talk is when it's about a case. And, if I try to bring up anything personal, you brush it off."

Frustrated that he wouldn't let it go, she put down her burrito. "What more is there to talk about? You know why we're not together."

"All I know is that you're being stubborn and refusing to give our relationship another chance."

"I told you before that I will not sit back and watch you die. Especially when you can just as easily prevent it."

"If I can save one more person, instead of cowering behind a desk like a chicken-shit, taking a bullet will be worth it to me."

He was so pigheaded and yet, it was why Carissa loved him. She just couldn't bear the thought of Dustin dying because of his stubbornness. Just like him, however, she wasn't one to back down. It was one of the reasons she'd left him in the first place. In her heart, she thought he'd eventually come to his senses and step away from his career. At least for her, if he wouldn't do it for himself. But she'd been wrong. The man was too headstrong for his own good.

"I know you want to save the world, but there are other things you could do that could be just as fulfilling."

He frowned. "Really? Like what?"

"What about the Cyber Crimes Center? You mentioned once that you were interested in trapping online pedophiles. Or, what about being a youth counselor? I mean, there has got to be something out there that keeps you out of the line of fire but can still give you purpose."

112

Dustin sighed wearily. "Carissa, did it ever occur to you that the future you see for me is going to happen, no matter what I do for a living? That the end result will occur because of every single choice I make in life, regardless of how I get there, or where the money in my wallet comes from?"

She opened her mouth to respond, but then realized he might very well have a point.

Oh, dear Lord....

What *if* the premonitions she had about Dustin were unstoppable?

The thought made her stomach sour.

She'd always assumed that the future could be changed. That her visions, these so-called gifts, were warnings. But what if they were inevitable outcomes? Unchangeable fates, written in stone?

Then I'm cursed and not gifted, she thought miserably.

Noticing Carissa's sudden silence and her troubled look, Dustin reached over and touched her cheek. "I love you, Carissa. I've never stopped," he said, staring into her eyes. "And as far as I'm concerned, my future has already been screwed because you don't want to be in it."

"But, I do," she replied, her eyes filling with tears. "I'm just so frightened of losing you."

"Babe, I'm here. Right now. You haven't lost me. Just… don't give up on me. On us."

Carissa blinked and tears rolled down her cheeks. Dustin wiped one away with his thumb.

"My God, woman. You're so busy mourning the 'dead' me, you're forgetting that I'm still alive and kicking." He smiled sadly. "And still hopelessly in love with you."

"I love you, too," she replied.

He leaned forward and kissed Carissa deeply, reminding her again of how much she'd missed and truly loved him. In those few

113

seconds, she knew that by continually asking him to give up something he was so passionate about, was totally unfair of her. And to give him an ultimatum, even crueler. *Her* stubbornness was the cause of both of their suffering. Not his.

"You're not getting rid of me so easily again," he said huskily when they pulled away. "Premonitions or not."

She smiled.

Dustin's stomach growled loudly, making them both laugh.

"Sorry," he replied, smiling sheepishly.

"No worries. Oh, speaking of premonitions, by the way, one is coming to me," Carissa replied with a straight face as he reached into the bag and grabbed another burrito. "Did you happen to bring some Tums?"

"Why?" he asked and then smiled. "Oh, one of us is going to be hating life soon?"

"It isn't going to be me," she said, as he reached for a salsa packet.

"Really?" With a devilish glint in his eyes, Dustin rolled up her window, which had been slightly cracked. "Think again."

AFTER THEY WERE finished eating, the two headed over to Jeremy's, in North Oaks.

"Wow, this is such a beautiful place," Carissa commented when they pulled up to the gated driveway. A tall metal fence surrounded the property, which seemed to be a block long.

He pulled out his phone. "You've never been here?"

"No."

Dustin sent Jeremy a text, and seconds later, the gate opened up. They slowly drove up to a massive colonial style mansion that looked more like a museum than a house.

"Looks like someone enjoys the holidays," Dustin remarked.

114

Colorful Christmas lights and expensive holiday decorations adorned the property; Carissa knew the amount of money spent on that alone would blow her mind.

"The government must have paid him well," she said.

"Yes, but his wife, Bria, also has money. Remember? She's a famous shoe designer."

"That's right," Carissa replied, remembering Jeremy had mentioned it once before, when the three of them had met for coffee. One pair of shoes cost more than what some paid for rent. It was outrageous. Although Carissa had a closet full of footwear, she couldn't fathom paying the kind of money they were charging for Bria Cole's line.

Dustin parked the car and the two went to the giant double-doors and knocked. A minute later, they opened up and Jeremy greeted them with a warm smile.

"It's good seeing you guys," he said, letting them in. "I mean, I know we talk on the phone, but it's not the same thing."

"True," Dustin said as they stepped into the grand foyer. "Wow, looks like Bria is really in the Christmas spirit this year, huh?"

Carissa couldn't help but stare at the enormous Christmas tree that stood between a double, winding staircase. Soft music, warm lighting, and more holiday decorations filled the area; it was almost like stepping into a Thomas Kinkade painting.

"Yes," he replied, glancing at the tree. "We're a little more festive than usual, though. She did an interview for some fashion magazine yesterday, and they took pictures of the house. That's why there's more decorations than usual."

"Well, it looks beautiful," Carissa said, smiling at Jeremy, in his dark, gray wool sweater and white turtleneck. As usual, he reminded her a professor she had in college, Mr. Duncan, with his messy red hair and thick beard.

115

"I'll let her know you thought so. She's a big fan of yours," Jeremy replied.

Carissa's eyes widened. "Really?"

"She's fascinated with your work and was frustrated when she found out you were going to be here. She's in New York right now," he answered. "Left this morning."

"Well, I'd love to meet her sometime," she said.

"We'll have to have you over for dinner." He looked at Dustin. "Both of you."

"That works for me," Dustin replied. "Does Bria still cook those fabulous meals or did you hire a chef?"

"Both." Jeremy looked Carissa. "When she's not cooking in the boardroom, she's cooking in the kitchen. I swear, she can't sit still. Always has to be doing something."

"I don't know much about women's shoes, but that wife of yours is an amazing cook," said Dustin.

"And it shows," Jeremy said, patting his waist.

"I was going to say, are you eating for two?" Dustin ribbed.

"Hopefully soon," he replied with a smirk. "We're working on expanding the family. Not just my waistline."

Dustin and Carissa laughed.

Jeremy sighed. "Anyway, I suppose we should get down to business and try to find the little girl. I actually may have found a couple of possible leads. Let's go to the den and I'll show you."

Carissa and Dustin followed him past the staircase to a long corridor that eventually led to his office.

"This is… new. How quaint," joked Dustin, as they stepped into what looked more like a library than office. "I think you should have gone bigger. It must get claustrophobic in such a small space."

Jeremy smirked. "I know. It's much more extravagant than what I'm used to. Hell, I was happy with my old office. But you

116

know Bria. When she decides on remodeling something, she goes overboard," he said, walking to his desk, where he had three separate computers set up, two desktops and one laptop. He sat down and began typing on the laptop. "Anyway, after hours of searching through filth, I happened upon a chatroom where two users were discussing some kind of auction. I tried asking questions, but they wouldn't divulge anything useful."

"Huh," said Dustin, folding his arms across his chest.

"I did some more checking, in another chatroom, and eventually learned who was hosting this event." Jeremy slid over to his other computer and pulled up a picture of a bald man in his thirties.

"Who is that?" Dustin asked.

"Yury Popov."

"You think he's selling kids?" he asked, leaning forward.

"He's certainly auctioning something the pedophiles were interested in. Anyway, one has to get a special invitation to participate in the auction, which I doubt I will have enough time to try and coordinate."

Dustin frowned. "Damn."

"The good news is, we believe that Popov might be linked to a Russian crime syndicate. One that specializes in human trafficking. So, there's a chance Lainey has been kidnapped by professionals, which it sounds like, our guy here is involved," Jeremy replied.

"And that's the good part?" Dustin muttered.

"No, the good part is that I checked with the airlines and it looks like Popov flew into Minneapolis about a week ago. We find him, and we might find Lainey."

Carissa, who'd been silent, stared at the man on the screen. "He's involved," she said, her stomach tingling. "I can feel it."

Dustin leaned forward. "Did you happen to find out when this auction is being held, Jeremy?"

117

"Friday night," he replied.

He nodded. "At least we have a little time. What about the boy, Sammy Johnson? Is it possible he might have been kidnapped by the same organization?"

Jeremy typed in something on the computer and Sammy Johnson's face pulled up. "I definitely think it's possible."

Carissa stared at the screen. Sammy was definitely a good-looking kid with his magnetic smile. "They're together. Lainey and Sammy," she said. "I'm pretty sure."

The two men looked at each other.

"We might be able to kill two birds with one stone here," said Dustin.

"Wouldn't that be great," Jeremy said with a grim smile.

"Is there anything else?" Dustin asked.

Jeremy smiled. "Oh, yeah. Ask and you shall receive." He handed him a piece of paper.

"What's this?" Dustin asked, staring at the writing.

"Exactly what it looks like. The make, model, and license plate number of the car Popov rented at the airport."

Dustin grinned. He slapped him on the back. "My man! I knew you'd come through for us."

Jeremy looked up at him. "Now, don't get too excited. We don't know where he's staying. But, I did place a call with the Minneapolis Police Department and spoke to one of my contacts there."

"You mean the police chief?" Dustin asked. "Fielding?"

"Oh," Jeremy gave him a funny smile. "I told you about him, huh?"

"Yeah. Last time we went out for drinks," he replied.

Jeremy grunted. "Remind me to stop at one the next time we go out. Anyway, Fielding put out an alert on this guy."

"You should call him and let him know that we think Sammy could be another victim of Popov's," Dustin said.

"I will," he replied.

"If Fielding asks, tell him it's *your* hunch though," Carissa said with a wry smile. "Something tells me he won't take it seriously if he believes a psychic is your source."

"Probably not. I'll tell him it was all me. Of course, if your information turns out to be correct, I'm going to make sure you get credit where it's due. Screw what Fielding thinks."

Carissa smiled.

"Hopefully, they'll locate Popov soon," Dustin said. "I would think he'd be staying at a local hotel or motel. What do you think, Carissa?"

"I don't know." Suddenly, an image of cornfields flashed through Carissa's mind. "Wait. I feel almost like he could be staying in a rural area. Possibly near a farm?"

"What about the children? Do you think they could be with him?" Dustin asked.

"I don't know… but," Carissa's eyes widened as another premonition hit her. One that caught her off guard. "I think I might have a clearer idea of who took Lainey."

Chapter 21

Lainey

TEN MINUTES LATER, Lainey, Tara, and Sammy approached a warm and inviting farmhouse. Christmas lights and holiday decorations lit up the porch and a welcoming mat wished them "Happy Holidays."

Tara pounded on the door, and eventually a thin, old man wearing faded blue bib overalls answered.

"Please, help us," begged Tara, relieved to see him.

Shocked, the farmer let them in and quickly started asking questions.

"We were kidnapped by some people staying at a nearby farmhouse," Tara explained.

"What?" he asked, his eyes becoming saucers.

Tara gave him some more details and then motioned toward Sammy and Lainey. "These two have even been on the news. You might have seen something about them."

Appalled by what she'd told him, he quickly called out for his wife. Seconds later, a heavyset woman holding a dish towel joined them, her face filling with concern when she noticed the three standing there.

"They say that they were kidnapped by those people renting Joe Dern's place," the farmer said angrily. "I knew something strange was going on over there. People coming and going at all hours of the night. Different vehicles. I thought maybe it was drugs, but this… this is pure madness."

The woman put a hand to her chest. "Oh, you poor things; you must be scared and freezing to death," she replied, looking down at their wet feet. "Edgar, we need to call the sheriff."

"Already on it," he said, rushing away.

The woman gave them a sympathetic smile. "Don't you worry about a thing. You're safe with us. My name is Wilma, by the way. What did you say your names were?"

Tara introduced them.

"Thank goodness you children got away. Your families must be worried sick. In fact, I remember seeing your mother on television, begging for your return," she said to Lainey. Wilma looked at Sammy. "And if memory serves me, an Amber Alert just went out for you." Wilma made the sign of the cross over her chest. "I have to say… this is surely a miracle that you were all able to escape."

Hearing Wilma speak of her mother, Lainey's eyes filled with tears. She missed her so much and had almost lost hope of ever seeing her again.

Noticing her crying silently, the woman clucked her tongue and gave her a warm hug. "You poor little thing, you must have been so terrified. All of you," she said, her eyes moving to Sammy and Tara.

"We were," Sammy replied. His eyes narrowed. "They were going to sell us!"

Looking horrified, the woman straightened up. "Well, that's not going to happen now. We aren't going to let any harm come to you," she said firmly. "Now, why don't you take off those wet

121

socks and come into the living room by the fire? I'll go and grab some blankets and then get you something warm to drink. Like hot cocoa. Would you like that?"

They all nodded.

"Wilma, did you pay the phone bill like I asked you?" Edgar called out from the other room. "It doesn't seem to be working."

"Yes, of course I did," she hollered back.

Edgar stepped back into the foyer. "The phone is dead," he said, looking worried.

Wilma's eyes widened in fear. She looked over at the children. "Lord have mercy. Could they have followed you?"

Suddenly, all the lights went off and Lainey cried out.

Trembling. Tara grabbed her hand and squeezed it. "Don't panic," she whispered.

"Edgar. Get the flashlights," said Wilma.

"Already on it," he replied, disappearing out of the room once more.

"I'm scared, Tara," Lainey whispered.

"Me too," Sammy said in a shaky voice.

"Everything is going to be okay," the woman said.

"I don't know what's going on, Wilma, but you'd better take them upstairs," said Edgar, returning with the flashlights.

"What are you going to do?" Wilma whispered sharply.

"What do you think I'm going to do? I'm going downstairs and get my gun," he replied.

Wringing her hands, Wilma moaned. "How can this be happening? Who *are* these horrible people?"

Edgar handed her a flashlight. "Woman, just get them upstairs like I told you," he replied gruffly before disappearing back down the hallway.

Wilma took a deep breath and released it. "I suppose it's possible this might just be a coincidence you showed up and the

122

power went off. We shouldn't panic," she said, forcing a smile to her face.

As if on cue, a loud crashing noise from outside made them all jump.

"What was that?" said Sammy, backing into Tara.

"It sounded like the trash can getting knocked over. Hopefully, we just have some hungry raccoons causing havoc," Wilma replied in a strained voice. "Anyway, we'd better get upstairs."

"Do either of you have a cell phone?" Tara asked as they made their way through the house. "Can't we just call the police?"

"My cell phone is in the car. In the glovebox. At least, I think. It's just one of those pay-as-you-go type of things, so I never hardly use it," she explained. "Edgar also has one somewhere, but the last time I checked, the battery was dead."

"Crap," Tara murmured.

"We're just simple country folk," Wilma explained. "We don't even use the internet, much less our cell phones."

As they were heading up the staircase, someone began pounding on the front door.

"Oh no!" squeaked Lainey, trying not to cry.

"Hurry, children," Wilma said, as their visitor stopped knocking and began to ring the doorbell insistently. She turned and pointed the flashlight down so they could see the steps better. "These are old and narrow. Be careful so you don't fall."

When they reached the top of the staircase, Wilma quickly led them to a walk-in closet located in hers and Edgar's bedroom.

"Hide in here," she said, opening the door. "Hopefully this will all be sorted out real soon. I'm going to go and check on Edgar and maybe see if I can find his cell phone. Whatever you do, don't leave the closet until I return, okay?"

They agreed.

123

"Here, why don't you take the flashlight," Wilma said, handing it to Tara. "I know this house like the back of my hand."

She grabbed it from her.

"Okay, then. I'll be back." Making another sign of the cross, Wilma quietly shut the door and left them alone.

"Tara," Lainey said, backing away from the door. "What if they get in and find us up here?"

"It will be okay. Edgar has a gun, remember?" Sammy said. "He can shoot them if he has to."

"What if they have guns?" Lainey asked, her eyes wide.

"They do," Tara said in a tight voice. She handed Sammy the flashlight. "Stay here. I'm going to go and look out the bedroom window. See if I can figure out what's happening outside."

"But she told us to stay in here," squeaked Lainey. "What if something happens to you?"

Tara put a hand on Lainey's shoulder. "I'm just going to have a quick look." She gave her a reassuring smile. "I'll be fine. Okay?"

Lainey stared at her but didn't say anything.

Tara gave them both a quick hug and then snuck out of the closet.

Chapter 22

Beth

DETECTIVE SAMUELS CALLED Beth back shortly after Carissa and Dustin left the house. He thanked her for the information regarding the repairman, and promised to have someone interview him.

"Also, the reporters are back," she told him, staring out the window.

"Really?"

"Yes." She cleared her throat. "They must have somehow found out about our meeting with Carissa Jones."

"Carissa Jones," he repeated. "Wait a second, you mean the psychic?"

"Yes. You know her?"

"We've met."

From the tone of his voice, Beth reasoned that he wasn't exactly a fan of hers.

"So, what did Ms. Jones have to say about your daughter?" he asked dryly

"She believes that the kidnapper has actually been in our house. In fact, that's how I remembered Bernie."

"Ah. Well, I can understand how you would want to try anything to locate your daughter. Just," he sighed, "don't put all of your eggs in her basket. You'll be disappointed."

"I take it you don't believe in psychics?"

"No. Sorry. Most of them are scam artists. The other ones are a few sandwiches short of a picnic."

Beth frowned. She liked Carissa and didn't think he was being fair. "Carissa didn't appear to be either of those. In fact, she helped find a missing girl up in Two Harbors last weekend. You must have heard about that?"

"Yeah. Look, Ms. Brown. I'm sure once in a while she stumbles upon something the police might have missed and I assure you, it's not because she has some kind of supernatural power. I understand why you'd want to try every angle in getting your daughter back. Just don't let yourself get swayed by any of her crazy ideas. And for God's sake, don't give her money."

"She didn't ask for any," Beth replied, feeling deflated. Although he wasn't insulting her, she felt like a child being scolded.

"That's a relief. Anyway, like I said, we'll look into the repairman and get back to you as soon as possible."

She didn't tell him that Carissa and Dustin were already on their way to check him out. Something told her Detective Samuels wouldn't be happy about it. Instead, she thanked him and that was the end of their conversation.

"WHAT DID SAMUELS say? Did he have anything new for us?" Tom asked. It was just the two of them in the kitchen. William and Helen had left to meet her daughter, who lived in Hudson, for dinner.

Beth shook her head and went over their conversation.

"So, he thinks she's a fruitcake?" Tom said, the look on his face telling her he was in agreement.

"Yes, but he's wrong," she said, frowning. "Carissa *has* a gift. I know you don't believe it, but when we were up in Lainey's room, she told me things she couldn't have known."

He opened his mouth to say something, but then changed his mind.

"What?" she asked, crossing her arms under her chest.

Tom sighed and ran a hand through his hair. "I'm just tired of arguing. If you think she's legit, then that's good enough for me."

Beth relaxed. She really didn't have the energy to argue and wanted to believe that Carissa could somehow help them find their daughter. It wasn't like the police were having any luck. Maybe she was grasping at straws, but at least it was something.

Beth sat down next to him at the table. "She is, Tom. I feel that if anyone can help us find Lainey, it's Carissa and Dustin."

"I don't care who finds her, as long as she's found," he replied, looking haggard.

She nodded in agreement.

He took a sip of coffee and stared out the kitchen window. "Honestly, I think Dustin seems to have his head on straight." He looked at her. "I'm glad your father hired him."

"Me, too."

Beth's phone began to ring. She jumped up and grabbed it from the counter, hoping it was Carissa.

"Who is it?" Tom asked.

"Mike."

His eyes hardened. Not saying anything, he looked away.

She answered the phone and walked out of the kitchen. Beth didn't always feel comfortable talking to Mike around Tom. In fact, there were times when she felt slightly guilty. She knew it was silly, but couldn't help it.

127

"Hi, babe," Mike said, sounding tired.

Hearing his voice was instantly comforting. "Hi. How are things going?"

"Okay. You sound better," he replied, a smile in his voice. "Have you heard any news about Lainey?"

"There's another suspect." Beth told him about Bernie.

"That's right! The repairman. I'm surprised we both forgot."

"If it wasn't for Carissa, I wouldn't have even thought about him."

"Carissa?"

She explained who she was.

"A psychic?" he asked. "That's... cool."

Unlike Tom, Beth knew Mike was more open-minded about most things, including the supernatural. It was one thing she loved about him.

"Yes. She's the same woman who located a missing girl up near Duluth. Did you hear about that?"

He told her he hadn't had time to watch much television.

"That's pretty impressive though, huh?" he said.

"Yes. Hopefully she can help us find Lainey." Beth then told him about Carissa and Dustin's friend, Jeremy, who worked for the government. "He's helping, too. Apparently, there is some kind of dark web where crooks buy and sell things, even children," she said, the idea making her physically ill. "Can you believe it?"

"I've heard about the dark web," he replied. "Never been on in, though."

"You need some kind of special software, I guess," she said.

"Huh. So, this Jeremy thinks he might be able to locate her through that? How?"

"Honestly, I really have no idea. But, you know the government. They have all kind of mad skills we have no clue about. Anyway, I'll let them worry about the 'how'. I just hope they can find her. Especially, before…" Beth paused.

"Before what?"

Her eyes filled with tears. "Carissa thinks someone is going to try and sell her on the dark web."

He let out a ragged sigh. "Wow. That's… a horrible thought."

"I know. I just pray they find her before it's too late."

"I'm so sorry, babe," he said softly.

"Me, too." Sniffling, she headed to the bathroom and grabbed a tissue. "Anyway, when are you coming home?"

"That's what I was calling you about. I'm on the road right now and should be back in a couple of hours."

She sighed in relief. "Thank God." Although he'd only been gone for a couple of days, Beth felt lost without him. Especially now.

"Keep me in the loop if you hear anything else, okay?"

"Will do. I love you."

"Love you, too. I'll see you soon," he replied.

They hung up and Beth splashed some cold water on her face. Grabbing a towel, she stared at her reflection in the mirror, wondering if the person who'd taken Lainey had stood where she now stood. Looked into the same mirror. Used her towels. The thought made her feel violated.

A loud knock on the door made Beth jump.

"You okay in there?" Tom asked.

"Yes," she said, relaxing. "You scared the daylights out of me."

"I'm sorry. I'm starving and was thinking about picking up some Asian food. Would you like some, too?"

She still wasn't very hungry, but knew she needed to stay healthy. At least for Lainey.

She opened the door. "Sure."

Tom stared down at her with concern. "You okay?"

129

"I won't be until we find her," she said softly.

"I know. I feel like we're both trapped in a nightmare together. This all seems so… surreal." Tom's eyes filled with tears. "I can't even imagine what our baby is going through."

"We'll find her," she replied, touching his shoulder.

Their eyes met and Beth could see the longing in his eyes. And not just for the return of their daughter. She removed her hand, the moment suddenly feeling a little too intimate. Too uncomfortable.

"Thanks for going to get food, by the way," she said, taking a step back.

"Of course." Shoving his hands into his pockets, he sighed. "I thought maybe we could talk, too, when I get back. There are some things I'd like to get off of my chest."

Beth's stomach knotted up. She'd seen the look in Tom's eyes and suspected he wanted to talk about the two of them. But, it was too late. She was engaged to someone else. As much as she still cared deeply for Tom, it was over between them. It had to be.

"What things?" she asked nervously.

He pulled out his car keys. "We can discuss it when I get back, if that's okay? I think I'll do better on a full stomach."

She forced a smile to her face. "Sure. Of course."

"By the way, what did Mike have to say?" he asked as they began walking down the hallway.

"He's returning earlier than planned."

His shoulders sagged. "Oh," he replied, sounding disappointed. "When is he getting back?"

"In a couple of hours."

"Hopefully he's finally getting his priorities straight," Tom mumbled. "I mean, who leaves the woman he loves at a time like this? I sure in the hell wouldn't."

Beth wanted to argue that Tom had no right to point fingers. He hadn't exactly put her and Lainey as a top priority when he'd

130

been gambling. But now was not the time to rehash the past and she was emotionally drained. So she held her tongue.

"So, do you still like shrimp lo mein?" he asked in the living room.

She smiled. "Yeah."

"Okay. By the way, I have to run a couple errands before I get back. It shouldn't take me too long," he replied, walking to the front door.

"Sounds good," she said.

Tom opened the door and stole another look her way before leaving. She wondered if he still planned on having the conversation with her and hoped not. They were both already hurting and she didn't need to cause him any more pain.

Chapter 23

Tara

TARA'S GUT TOLD her she'd made a terrible mistake by involving the friendly old couple. Even though Edgar had a gun, nobody was as evil and ruthless as Yury and Kurt. The two kind strangers would probably get killed and it would be her fault.

Upset and angry with herself, Tara hurried over to the window and peered down below. Sure enough, Kurt's vehicle was parked outside. She backed away, wondering what to do. She knew that hiding in the closet and waiting for the inevitable, which would be their captors finding them, wasn't in their best interests.

I have to think of something.

The sound of splintering wood made her jump.

Terrified, Tara rushed back into the closet.

"What was that noise?" asked Lainey, staring at her wide-eyed.

Tara guided them toward the back of the closet. "They're getting into the house. Get behind the clothing. I'll hide you."

Tara knew it was only a matter of time before they'd be found and she needed to do something quickly.

The children did as Tara instructed and she did her best to cover them up with Wilma's long dresses.

"What are *you* going to do?" Sammy asked.

132

"I'm going to try and lead them away," she whispered, pushing a box of old clothing in front of them to help conceal their feet. "Whatever you do, don't leave the closet unless I come for you. Okay?"

Realizing what she was saying, Lainey gasped. "No. Stay here with us," she begged, peeking out at her from between the clothing. "If they catch you, they'll hurt you."

"Don't worry about me," Tara said. "Just do what I say and *please* don't leave the closet, no matter what you hear."

Lainey looked terrified. "But—"

A loud crash and then the sound of a gun firing made them all freeze. Following the noise, they heard Wilma crying out her husband's name.

"They shot her!" Sammy sobbed.

"No," moaned Lainey.

Tara wasn't sure who'd been shot, but something told her that if she didn't act soon, the next bullet might be headed her way.

"Please, you guys. You have to stay quiet," she pleaded. "And don't you dare come out. Do you understand?"

They both answered "yes."

Taking a deep breath, Tara slipped out of the closet and quietly crept toward the bedroom door. As she took her last step, the floorboard creaked loudly.

Her stomach dropped.

Terrified, she waited for someone to come charging through the doorway.

"Oh no, my poor Edgar!" screamed Wilma shrilly from downstairs. "You horrible, horrible, man! You shot my husband!"

Trembling, Tara opened the door as quietly as possible. As she stepped out of the bedroom, she could hear Kurt and Yury threatening to kill Wilma if she didn't give them up.

"I don't know what you're talking about," she sobbed. "Please, let me call an ambulance. My husband is *dying*."

"Tell us where those kids are first," demanded Kurt. "We saw their footsteps leading to your porch. We know they're here. Where are they, upstairs?"

"I don't know who you're talking about. What kids?" lied Wilma.

There was a loud slapping noise and the older woman gasped in pain.

"You still going to play games?" Yury asked angrily.

The woman didn't answer. She just continued to cry.

Tara's guilt ate her up inside. They were going to kill Wilma and she was to blame. It made her want to do something— anything, to help her. But then she remembered the excruciating pain Yury had inflicted on Tara the last time she'd escaped. This time, he'd surely torture and kill her. Along with Wilma.

Yury grunted. "Stupid, old bat. Kurt, go and check upstairs. I'll take a look down below."

"What about her?"

In answer, Tara heard another gunshot, startling her.

"There. Any more questions?" Yury replied in a satisfied voice.

Tears filled Tara's eyes as she realized what he'd done. She covered her mouth in horror.

Kurt swore. "You could have warned me," he snapped. "Now I have blood on my shoes."

"Pfft. Your fault for standing so close," replied Yury. "Now, go upstairs."

Panicking, Tara backed away from the staircase and ran to the other bedroom. She quietly shut the door and went over to the window. Looking outside, she sighed in relief. If she was careful, she could crawl down to the lower part of the roof, to the veranda. From there, she decided that she should be able to make it to the

134

patio below without getting hurt. At least she hoped. Regardless, it was her only option.

"Children! We know you're here. You'd better get your asses out here before someone else gets hurt!" hollered Kurt, his voice getting closer.

Praying that Lainey and Sammy wouldn't obey him, she threw open the window, knocked out the screen, and climbed out, making as much noise as possible. Just as Tara hoped, Kurt followed the sounds to her.

"Hey, get back here!" he growled angrily, sticking his head out the window as she climbed and slid down the wet, slippery roof.

Ignoring him, Tara continued her descent until she was hanging from one of the veranda beams. Taking a deep breath, she dropped to her feet, landing hard, but without injury.

Kurt pointed his gun down at her. "Stop right there and don't move."

Tara needed him to believe that the children were already outside. She turned toward the woods and cupped her mouth. "Keep running, you guys! Don't stop!"

Falling for it, Kurt swore and disappeared back inside.

Sighing in relief, she took off around to the back, praying Kurt would assume she'd followed Sammy and Lainey away from the house.

Chapter 24

Hawk

HAWK STARED AT Kurt's text message in anger. Both the children had escaped, and he knew that if by some miracle they made it to the police, he was royally screwed. Desperate to make sure *that* didn't happen, he raced to the farmhouse, hoping that by the time he arrived, Yury and Kurt would have the situation under control. Unfortunately, when he walked inside, the only person around was Dina.

"What happened to you?" he asked, noticing she was holding a rag against the side of her head. There was also dried blood under her nose.

"Bitch hit me in head with lamp," she snapped and then began complaining in Russian.

"Tara hit you?" he asked, a little surprised she'd gotten the upper hand with Dina.

"Yes."

He sighed. Kurt always had a soft spot for Tara, which he'd warned him about before.

"This is all Kurt's fault," Dina said, glaring at him. "He let her get away with too much, and now… they are gone."

Dina hated Tara. He wasn't exactly sure why, considering both had once been kidnapped as children. And if anything, Tara was more of a prisoner than Dina, who could now come and go with permission. It didn't mean she was free, however. So why she hated Tara, who had far less freedom than she did, was beyond him.

"How did they escape?" he asked. "On foot?"

"Yes. Kurt and Yury will bring them back."

Not so sure about that, he turned and headed back out to his truck. He was furious at the turn of events. Not only was he in danger of getting arrested, but he hadn't yet been paid for abducting Lainey and Sammy. Then there was the matter of the snoopy psychic, Carissa Jones. He'd seen her on television a couple times, and knew the woman was either very lucky, or truly did have a gift. If it was the latter, and she was able to connect him to the kidnapping, shit could really hit the fan. He couldn't have that.

Starting up his vehicle, he turned it around and began driving slowly away from the house, almost wishing he'd never gotten involved in the trafficking racket in the first place. But, he *was* good at what he did, and the money he received made the dangers associated with the kidnapping tolerable. Unfortunately, it was getting harder and harder to get his hands on the kind of merchandise Yury wanted, and… not any ol' child would do. They had to have that special 'look'. One of innocence and beauty. The kind of look that made the rich freaks open up their wallets. Like beautiful, delicate little Lainey.

Sighing in irritation, he regretted ever showing Yury his cell phone. But the Russian had insisted on going through it to see what kind of man they were doing business with. Upon seeing a picture of Lainey, he'd started asking questions.

"She would bring us a huge payday," the Russian had said, handing him back his wallet. "And, would prove your loyalty to us."

"Are you insane?" he'd replied, shocked at the request.

"Everyone has a price. Give me yours."

At first, he'd scoffed at the very idea of giving them Lainey. But then Yury had made a ridiculous offer. One a guy like him, who already had a first class ticket to Hell, could not refuse.

Chapter 25

Carissa

WHEN THEY ARRIVED back at Beth's place, they found her alone.

"So, what did you learn?" she asked, letting them in. "I've been waiting on pins and needles."

"Sorry," Carissa said as they stepped into her living room. "I wanted to talk to you in person." She looked around. "Where's Tom?"

Beth waved her hand. "Oh, he had a couple errands to run, and then was going to bring back some Chinese food."

"Where's William?" asked Dustin.

"He's out with Helen visiting her daughter. Why?" she asked. Her eyes it up. "Did you learn something new?"

"Actually, I think so," Carissa said softly.

There was an awkward tension in the air. Beth's eyes darted back and forth from Carissa to Dustin. She smiled nervously. "Well, what is it? I'm going crazy here."

"You should probably sit down," Carissa said.

"You're making me nervous," Beth said, walking over to the sofa. "Somehow, I don't feel as if you're about to give me good news."

Carissa followed her over and sat down next to her. "Sorry. I, um," she let out a sigh, "I think I've finally figured out who the man was at Walmart."

Beth looked relieved. "Was it that repairman, Bernie?"

Carissa shook her head. "I think it's someone close to you." She cleared her throat. "How long have you known Mike?"

"Mike?" Beth repeated, staring at her in disbelief. "*My* Mike? You don't think…" She put a hand against her chest. "No way. He would never be involved in something like this."

"Let's hope that you're right," Dustin said.

Carissa agreed. She didn't want to outright accuse him of anything without proof.

"I am right," Beth said angrily.

"Do you have a picture of Mike?" Carissa replied, wishing she didn't feel so strongly about Beth's fiancé. But, she'd sensed early on that the person might be close to Beth and she'd already ruled out Tom. She just needed something to confirm her suspicions and then figure out where to go from there.

"Yes, I do," Beth said, reaching over to grab her phone from the end table. She began scrolling through her photos. "I still think you're way off-course, though. Mike is a kind and loving man. He loves Lainey and would never do her any harm. Besides," she glanced up, "he has a son of his own. How could a man like that be involved in something so sordid?"

Carissa wanted to tell her about the serial killer she'd once met who'd also been a family man. His children had loved him dearly and had no idea of the true monster he'd been. Nor his wife, who'd been shocked when he'd been arrested for murder and later found guilty of torturing and killing six women. But, she didn't think it would help the situation.

"I'm sorry. It's always possible my visions aren't totally clear or I'm reading them wrong. But if Mike is involved, and we don't check him out, your daughter could be lost to us forever."

Sighing, Beth turned her phone around and showed Carissa a picture of him. "This is Mike. I don't have many of him, unfortunately. He hates having his picture taken."

"May I?" Carissa asked politely.

"Go ahead," Beth replied, holding the cell phone out to her.

She took it and stared at the man in the photo. He reminded her a little of the actor, Ted Danson, in his younger years. He certainly didn't look like a child predator, but evil came in many different forms.

"Well?" asked Dustin, sitting across from them.

Carissa looked at him. "I don't know, but… I really think we need to check him out."

Beth's face turned stormy. "I don't believe it. I *won't* believe it."

"I understand how difficult this is and I hope, for your sake, that I'm wrong and he's not involved," Carissa said softly, handing her the phone back.

"You *are* wrong. In fact, he's coming home soon. You can see for yourself that Mike is one of the sweetest men in the world. He loves me. He loves Lainey," Beth replied, looking ready to burst into tears.

"I'm sorry, Beth. You might be right about him, but I also know you'd move mountains to find your daughter. I think it's important to put aside your feelings until we know for sure that he isn't involved."

She let out a ragged sigh. "Fine."

"Where exactly was Mike when Lainey was kidnapped?" Dustin asked.

"Colorado," Beth said, leaning back in the sofa. "As I mentioned before, he was at an art convention."

141

"Do you know the name of the hotel where he stayed?" Carissa asked.

"I think he said it was the Hilton," she replied.

"Why don't you give me Mike's cell phone number and we'll have Jeremy do some digging. By the way, has he ever mentioned the name Yury Popov?" asked Dustin.

"No," she replied, watching as he took out a pen and small notepad. "Why? Who is he?"

They explained that Popov was connected to Russian mafia, and is believed to be involved with human trafficking.

"Do you think he has Lainey?" she asked, her face pale.

"It's a very good possibility, but he's definitely not the person on the Walmart video," Dustin said. "Popov is twice that man's size and very muscular."

"Well, I've never heard the name before," Beth replied and then grabbed her phone again. She pulled up Mike's phone number and gave it to him.

"And where is he supposed to be now?" Dustin asked, scribbling the number down.

"On his way back," she replied, looking at the time, "from Madison. He should be here in about an hour."

"Okay. Let me get this information to Jeremy and we'll see if he can verify that Mike really was in Colorado the day Lainey disappeared, and if he's used his credit card anywhere in Wisconsin the last couple of days." Dustin took out his cell phone and began dialing.

Beth looked at Carissa, a tortured expression on her face. "If he's involved, I just don't know if I'll be able to handle it."

"You will. Your daughter needs you to," she replied softly.

Chapter 26

Lainey

AFTER TARA LEFT, Lainey and Sammy heard Kurt calling out for them.

"Children! We know you're inside. You'd better get your asses out here before someone else gets hurt!"

His voice grew closer and Lainey began to whimper in fear.

"Shush," whispered Sammy, also frightened. "They'll hear you."

She put her hand over her mouth and closed her eyes, expecting that any minute, the closet door would open up and Kurt would find them.

"Yury! They're outside!" hollered Kurt suddenly.

Lainey didn't understand exactly what was happening, but she could hear Kurt's footsteps as he raced down the hallway and farther away.

"Who's outside?" whispered Lainey, confused.

"I don't know. Maybe he saw Tara?" he replied.

"He said 'they'. Not 'her'," Lainey replied.

He didn't reply.

"What if it's the cops?"

Sammy sighed. "I doubt it."

They waited, both confused and unsure of where Tara had run off to and what to do. Suddenly, the closet door opened quickly, startling both of them.

It was Tara.

"Come on. Let's go," she whispered, moving items out of the way so they could get out.

Relieved, Lainey pushed the clothes away and stepped forward. "Is it safe? Are the cops here?"

"No. I wish. Gary and Yury think we've left, though," she replied.

"Then, shouldn't we stay?" Sammy asked.

"No, because when they realize we haven't left, they'll be back. Let's go," she said.

Lainey didn't want to leave the safety of the closet, but was too terrified of them finding her. "Okay."

"I'm not leaving," whispered Sammy stubbornly. "I mean, where are we supposed to go? And, what about Edgar and Wilma?"

"They're both dead," Tara replied grimly.

Lainey gasped.

Sammy's eyes widened. "Then… they're going to kill us, too, aren't they?" he said, his voice cracking.

"You're young and worth more to them alive. I've already disobeyed them once before," said Tara. "Yury will kill me this time."

Lainey's eyes filled with tears at the thought of Tara dying. "Don't say that," she whispered. "I don't want them to hurt you."

Staring at her, a determined look crossed Tara's face. She gave her a reassuring smile. "Don't worry. We're all going to get out of this alive. I'll do whatever it takes. Okay?"

Lainey nodded.

"I still think we should stay hidden up here," Sammy said in a grumpy voice.

"The next time they show up, they'll search the entire house, including this closet. I have an idea. We need to find one of Edgar or Wilma's cell phones. We'll call the cops and hide in the woods until help arrives. It shouldn't take them too long to get here."

"But, aren't *they* in the woods looking for us?" Sammy asked.

"Let me go and take a peek outside," she said, stepping out of the closet again. "Stay here."

Lainey and Sammy looked at each other.

"I can't believe they killed the old couple," Lainey said. "They were so nice."

He nodded.

Tara re-entered the closet. "I don't see Kurt's car out there anymore. They must be heading back toward the road again, thinking we did, too. We need to do something now, while we still can."

"Okay. Fine," Sammy said, still pouting.

"Wait." Tara looked through the hangers. She grabbed a green flannel shirt and a white sweater. "Here," she said, handing them out. "Put these on. At least you'll be a little warmer."

Lainey pulled the sweater over her pajamas while Sammy put on the flannel shirt. Meanwhile, Tara rushed over to the old couple's dresser. She opened up several drawers until she found the one she needed.

"Put these on," Tara said, tossing the children dry, warm socks.

"More socks?" said Sammy.

"It's all we have. I doubt you can fit into Edgar's or Wilma's shoes," said Tara.

They sat down on the carpeting and quickly did as she asked. Afterward, the three crept out of the bedroom and down the staircase with Tara holding the flashlight. At the bottom of the steps they found Wilma and Edgar, motionless. Even in the darkness, they could see there was blood everywhere, including the walls; it looked like something out of a horror movie.

"Gnarly," Sammy mumbled, his face turning greenish-white. He grimaced. "I think I'm going to get sick."

Horrified, and feeling pretty ill herself, Lainey quickly looked away from the dead bodies. "Those poor people," she moaned.

"I know. Come on," Tara said, holding out her hand with a sad expression. "Just, try not to look at them."

Swallowing the lump in her throat, Lainey grabbed Tara's hand and stepped around the old couple. Shuddering, Sammy quickly followed.

When they reached the living room, Tara peeked outside and sighed. "Their car is still gone," she whispered.

"What now?" Sammy asked, looking relieved.

Tara turned around. "Look for a cell phone. Didn't Wilma say she thought Edgar's was in the kitchen?"

Sammy nodded. "Yeah, but she also mentioned it was probably dead."

"True, but they must have a charger somewhere. Let's go," she replied.

TARA LED THEM into the kitchen, where they looked around in the dark, too frightened to use the flashlight. Instead of the cell phone, however, they found a set of car keys dangling on a hook.

"Okay, new plan," Tara said, grabbing them. "I think these are the keys to the vehicle I saw parked out back. It might be our way out of here."

"What if they see us?" Sammy asked.

Tara was silent for a few seconds and then said, "I'll drive without the headlights on. Come on."

146

They snuck through the kitchen's sliding glass door and went outside to the back of the house where there was an old, yellow Chrysler parked. Lainey slid into the back and Sammy got in front with Tara.

"Will it even start?" Sammy asked, rubbing his damp feet.

"Let's hope so. Look in the glovebox for a phone, will ya?" Tara said.

"Okay," he replied, opening it up.

Holding her breath, Tara stuck the key into the ignition. When the engine turned over, she let out a sigh of relief.

"Thank goodness," Sammy said.

Tara looked around, worried that the sound of the car starting would attract attention. Although Kurt's car was gone, she was still on edge. One of them could have stayed back, looking for them.

"Hey, I found her phone," said Sammy, holding it up. "It's dead, though."

"Try to find a charger," Tara said, looking around the dashboard at the controls. She bit her lower lip. "Damnit."

"What is it?" Sammy asked, looking up from the cell phone.

"Uh, nothing," she replied.

He frowned. "Haven't you ever driven before?"

"No." Tara tried shifting the car into DRIVE, but the lever wouldn't budge. "Obviously, I didn't get out much."

"Yeah, I suppose not. Um, I think you have to put your foot on one of those pedals while you do that," said Sammy, pointing downward.

"Okay." Tara pressed on the brake, shifted into DRIVE, and then moved her foot to the gas pedal. They lurched forward until she stomped on the brake. "Sorry," she said, looking back at Lainey, who'd tumbled down to the floor-boards. "You okay?"

"Yes," Lainey replied, crawling back up onto the seat.

147

"You'd better put your seatbelt on," Tara said. She glanced over at Sammy. "Put yours on, too, Sammy."

He pulled the strap over his chest and buckled the seatbelt.

"I suppose I should back this thing up before we crash into the house," Tara mused.

"Yeah. I was going to say…" Sammy replied with a smirk.

TARA'S HEART POUNDED madly in her chest as they drove away from the farmhouse. She couldn't believe that after all this time, she might actually truly be… free.

Her thoughts went back to when she'd first met Kurt, which had been online in a gaming chatroom. At the time, she'd lived in North Dakota with her mother and siblings. He'd lied and told her he was twelve. He'd acted the part perfectly, even showing her his online profile, which had been fake. After about a month of chatting and playing online games together, Kurt mentioned that he was going to be in town, visiting relatives, and had asked to meet up at a nearby park. The naïve fool she'd been, Tara had agreed without doubt or hesitation; that's when her life took a horrible turn. Forced into a van by Kurt and his group, which she'd never seen coming, Tara had been an easy victim.

From that day forward, her life became a living nightmare. Not only did Kurt sexually abuse her, but he took nude pictures of Tara to sell on the web. If that wasn't bad enough, he developed some kind of sick, twisted love for her, which ended up working for and against Tara. Because of this, she wasn't sold like most of their victims, but kept a captive and eventually given special treatment for being complacent. In other words, Tara found a way to mentally block out the horrible things taking place while they happened. She would go to her special place until Kurt was finished and try to pretend that it never happened. Eventually, as

148

she grew older and became more womanly, his interest in Tara waned until he no longer touched her at all. That's when she was forced into assisting with the younger children.

Tara pictured the seven-year-old girl she'd tried escaping with soon after. It was the time Yury had beaten her, making sure she never tried pulling the stunt again. That had been three years ago. Now, here she was again, only this time… things were looking up. At least, she hoped. As far as the old couple, Tara felt sick about their deaths. She had to believe that saving Lainey and Sammy would somehow be worth it in the end.

"Where did Yury and Kurt go?" Lainey suddenly asked from the backseat.

"I really don't know," Tara replied, searching for their headlights in the distance. "Hopefully back to the farm."

"Or maybe they're waiting for us somewhere ahead," said Sammy.

"Let's hope not," she mumbled.

Chapter 27

Hawk

HE MET UP with Kurt and Yury on the dirt road. Hawk rolled down his window. "See any sign of them?" he asked.

"Yeah, we tracked them down to a neighboring farmhouse but they escaped again," Kurt replied angrily. "I think they could be in the woods somewhere."

Hawk swore.

"That's not even the worst part," Kurt said. "We had to shoot the meddling old couple who lived there. They saw the kids and tried to help them."

"Yes. The shit has hit the fan. We need to find these brats and move before someone discovers the bodies," Yury said, leaning around Kurt to look at him.

Kurt took out a cigarette and lit the end. "Exactly. The last thing we need is for the cops to come snooping around our farmhouse, and you know they will."

"Of course they will, you idiot," added Yury, looking disgusted. "Even if we clean up the mess, we still have to move the operation now."

Kurt frowned.

"The kids can't get too far," Hawk said, looking out into the darkness. It was cold, wet, and there wasn't another house around

150

for least a couple of miles. He tapped his thumbs on the steering wheel. "I'll head back toward the main road again and veer back."

"Bring me back to farmhouse," Yury said. "I need pack up some things while you two look for the runaways."

"Okay," Kurt replied.

Hawk rolled up his window and drove slowly toward the main road, his eyes scouring the line of trees surrounding him. When he reached the main frontage road, he turned the truck around and drove back the way he'd come. Although he tried to remain calm, his mind was spinning. He knew if Lainey made it to the police and squealed, he'd have to skip town. Fortunately, he'd been smart and had stowed away some emergency cash. There was also the offshore account he had, which couldn't be traced back to him. He had a good chunk of money there, too. Good thing he'd been smart enough to plan ahead for something like this. Still, the idea of running and leaving everything behind was annoying.

He should have never agreed to Lainey.

Hawk thought about Beth and how furious she'd be. How shocked and hurt she would be when she found out he'd been involved. Oddly enough, he felt no remorse or empathy toward the situation. Feelings were more of an enigma to him than anything. His family would be shocked if they knew what went on in his head. Or what didn't. The only thing that gave him any kind of pleasure was the thrill of kidnapping and cold, hard cash. Hell, if the price was right, he'd even consider selling Mason. Part of him would enjoy it, especially when having to face the police. He loved games, and the best kind were risky and dangerous. He'd always been the cat, but admittedly, being the mouse sounded a little provocative. The thought gave him goosebumps.

Maybe I should toss the police a few breadcrumbs, he thought in amusement.

151

Of course, in the end, they wouldn't catch him. Even if they realized he was involved. Which was why he knew he wouldn't offer the police any clues. It would be a waste of time and he couldn't afford to have his buyers behind bars. He loved the setup they had. They offered him everything he craved—high risk and a shitload of money. It gave him a high. Almost like Heroin. And once the thrill flickered out—and it always did once a job was finished—he craved more. More danger. More risk. Which was why, even though he was frustrated the children had escaped, he was also buzzing with excitement. He almost hoped Kurt wouldn't find the kids. He wanted to be the one to track them down. *Needed* to be the one.

Chapter 28

Tara

"DO WE GET to go home now?" asked Lainey.

"Not yet. We're going to the police station," Tara replied, knowing it would be too dangerous to try and take them home right away. Kurt and Yury could have someone stationed there, waiting. Tara knew how much money was on the line and they wouldn't just walk away without trying to somehow intercept Lainey and Sammy.

"By the way, did you find a charger for the phone?" she asked Sammy as the car crept further down the private road.

"No," he said.

"That's okay," she replied. "At least we have the car."

Oddly enough, Tara was a little apprehensive of what might happen at the police station. She didn't know where she'd go afterward or who would take care of her. Probably Juvie or foster care. She doubted her mother would want her back. From what Kurt had said, she hadn't put in any effort to try and find her.

"Most parents try to locate their missing kids. They get on the news. They put up posters. But, your mother didn't do any of that," he said, after she tried escaping the first time. *"So, where would you even go? Nobody wants you. Nobody but me. I'm the only family you've got now."*

Tara thought about her mom, Carol, and her younger sister and brother, Annie and Sean. Carol had been a single mother,

153

working two jobs trying to support everyone. When she hadn't been working or running them around, she'd been taking online college courses. Always busy, Carol hadn't objected to Tara's internet usage. In fact, she'd seemed relieved that Tara had something to keep her occupied. The thought that she hadn't put any effort into finding her hurt.

"I can't wait to go home," said Lainey as they drove back to the fork-in-the-road. "I need to tell my mother about—"

"Tara!" hollered Sammy, pointing toward the farmhouse they'd escaped from. "There they are!"

Sure enough, Kurt and Yury were almost at the farmhouse, their taillights glowing in the dark. Frightened, she quickly took a right and headed in the opposite direction

"Did they see us?" she asked Sammy, keeping her attention on the road in front of them.

"I... I don't know," he replied, looking back over his shoulder. "I can't tell."

Fear slithered under her skin, making her break out into a cold sweat. She knew Kurt or Yury would see them soon enough if she didn't put some distance between them.

"Hold on, you guys," she said, pressing harder on the gas.

The gravel road was icier than ever, and with her inexperienced driving, they almost ended up in a ditch. Trying to remain calm, she slowed down, glancing occasionally in the rearview mirror. Fortunately, Kurt's taillights seemed to be getting farther away.

Tara let out the breath she'd been holding "Maybe they didn't notice us."

"They're getting farther away," said Lainey, also looking out the rear window.

She checked again. The lights were all but disappeared now, the distance between them growing wider.

"You guys, I think… I think we actually did it," Tara said, her eyes filling with tears of joy. "We've… escaped."

The two children began to cheer.

"Don't celebrate yet," she said, smiling and wiping the corner of her eye. "We may have escaped, but I'm driving. So… we're still in a lot of danger."

"You're doing great!" Sammy said. "Especially for someone who's never driven."

"Thanks. Actually, I used to ride four-wheelers at my aunt's cabin and that probably helped." Aunt Joan had been related to her father, who'd died of cancer when she was nine. Tara remembered how much fun they'd had and wondered if she'd ever get to see her again.

"What's a four-wheeler?" Lainey asked.

As she was explaining, Tara kept checking the rearview mirror. Her heart was still racing and knew they weren't out of the woods yet. They still had another half mile or so to go before they reached a real paved road. This felt almost like a scene from a horror flick and she knew what happened to movie characters who let their guard down. Nothing good.

"That sounds like fun," said Sammy. "I've never been on one."

"You'd have a blast," Tara said, grateful the moon was out and the layer of snow that had accumulated seemed to help her see better. "Maybe, if things work out, I can invite you over to my aunt's." Her heart stopped. There was suddenly a vehicle headed toward them.

"Oh, my God, who is that?"

"Maybe it's one of the other neighbors. Or a cop?" Sammy said.

Tara didn't think it was a cop.

"You guys, get down," she ordered.

"Shouldn't we see if they can help us?" Sammy asked.

155

"No. It might be one of *them*," Tara said, her voice quivering. Although she'd never met the others involved with the trafficking, she knew they were out there. "Now, unbuckle and get down so they don't see you."

The children did as she asked and slid down to the floor mats. Taking a deep breath, Tara turned on the headlights, so the other driver wouldn't run into them, and continued forward. She didn't know what else to do, but understood that there wasn't any other route to take.

Please, help us…

As the vehicle grew nearer, Tara tried to stay calm, but the truth was, she was trembling like crazy and about ready to pee her pants.

Sammy looked up at her. "Who is it? Can you tell?"

"Not yet," she answered, clutching the steering wheel tightly.

When it was almost upon them, the other vehicle flashed its high beams, momentarily blinding her. Gasping, she stomped on the brake without thinking. The wheels spun and Tara lost control of the car.

Chapter 29

Hawk

HAWK NOTICED A pair of lights suddenly appear in the distance. At first, he thought it might be Kurt, but as the car grew closer, he realized that the headlights were different. Since there weren't any other houses around, besides the old couple's—and Kurt mentioned they were now dead—Hawk knew it could only mean one thing. Tara had gotten her hands on a car.

Impressed at her ingenuity, he waited until the vehicle was close and then turned on his high beams.

The other driver, definitely Tara, swerved and lost control of the car. It slid off the road and ended up down in the ditch.

Pleased with himself, Hawk parked the truck and slid a ski mask over his face. Grabbing his gun, he noticed she was trying to get the car free. But the harder she tried, the more stuck the Chrysler became. It amused him.

Whistling to himself, he walked over to the driver's side door and rapped on the window.

Tara looked at him, her eyes wide with fear.

"Unlock the door!" he ordered.

Ignoring him, she tried throwing the car into reverse again, which kicked up snow and mud.

Pissed off, Hawk raised the gun and pointed it at the window. Knocking on the glass again, he made sure she saw it.

"Unlock it now!" he yelled, cocking the pistol.

Frightened, but not completely stupid, she did as he asked.

Hawk opened the door and grabbed her by the arm, pulling her outside roughly. She slipped and fell down into the snow. Meanwhile, he could hear the children crying out for her in the vehicle.

"Get up," he ordered.

Weeping, Tara got back onto her feet.

"Do you know how much trouble you've caused?" he asked angrily, holding the gun up to her face. "*Do* you?"

"I'm sorry," she said, sobbing.

Although he'd never shot anyone before, his finger itched to pull the trigger. She'd made a mess of things and knew Kurt wouldn't have the heart to kill her, and of course, he'd beg Yury to keep her alive.

But he knew Tara was too dangerous to their setup. She'd almost gotten away this time, and if given the chance, would try it again.

"Please don't kill me," she begged.

Sighing, Hawk lowered the gun to her thigh. He didn't have time to deal with her, but didn't want her running off.

"Sorry, but… this is going to hurt," he said before pulling the trigger.

Chapter 30

Carissa

"WHAT DID JEREMY have to say?" she asked Dustin after he hung up the phone.

"Not too much. I gave him Mike's phone number and hotel information," he replied. "He said he'll check on it."

"Okay," she replied.

"I think we should go. It's getting late," Dustin said quietly. "I'm sure she probably needs some time to herself anyway. That bombshell you laid on her was definitely a hard thing to swallow."

Carissa glanced over at Beth, who was on her phone, talking to Detective Samuels again. "I know, but... I'd like to meet Mike first. He should be arriving soon, from what she said."

"Sure. We can wait."

They walked over to the sofa and sat down together, waiting for Beth to finish her conversation. When she did, Dustin asked if the detective had any new leads.

Beth sighed. "No, although he also asked me about the guy you mentioned. Yury Popov. He wanted to know if I'd ever heard the name before."

"Samuels must have spoken to Fielding," Dustin said to Carissa.

She nodded.

159

"Who's that?" Beth asked, sitting down.

"He's the Minneapolis police chief. Jeremy and Fielding are longtime acquaintances, so he reached out to him," Dustin explained.

Beth looked relieved. "So, now maybe Lainey will get the attention she deserves. Not that Samuels isn't a good cop. He just doesn't seem like he's doing enough."

"Samuels *is* a good cop, but he could definitely be doing better," Carissa said, still remembering their first encounter. "I've dealt with him before."

"Really?" Beth asked. "Another case?"

She nodded and told her about it.

Last summer, a nine-year-old boy had been abducted while riding his bike home from a friend's house in Forest Lake. It had been around eight o'clock in the evening and the man who picked him up, Joe Phillips, had been a longtime neighbor. Stephen had trusted the man, so when he was told that his mother needed him to come home quickly because of a family emergency, the little boy hadn't thought twice about getting into his truck.

"A neighbor?" repeated Beth, surprised. "That's crazy."

"What's crazy is that it happens all the time," Dustin said. "Many times the child trusts the perpetrator. In fact, they usually spend time grooming them before they actually make a move. In that case, Stephen looked at him only as a friendly neighbor."

"How did you get involved?" Beth asked Carissa. "Did you know the family personally?"

"No," replied Carissa.

The fact was, she wasn't even sure how or why she'd envisioned what would happen to that particular boy. It wasn't as if she'd come into any physical contact with him or his family, which usually triggered her premonitions. But two hours after the boy had gone missing, an Amber Alert went out and she'd been watching

160

television when they'd broadcasted it. The moment she saw the photo of Stephen, she immediately called the police.

"I know who has the little Cutler boy," she'd told the operator on the phone.

They'd immediately connected her to Detective Samuels, who, coincidently, was a friend of the missing boy's family. When she told him of her vision, he'd said a few choice words, and then hung up on her. Knowing that it was a matter of life or death, she drove her SUV to the neighborhood where the search party was looking for the child, and was able to talk to the boy's uncle, Tim.

"There's a fifty-something-year-old man who lives in this neighborhood. He owns a white pickup truck and always wears a fishing hat," she'd told him desperately. "He's taking Stephen to his cabin."

"How do you know this?" the uncle had asked, skeptical.

"I saw him take the boy," she'd said, which had been both a lie and the truth. "You have to hurry and stop him before he kills your nephew. Believe me, he will if you don't do something."

Frantic, Tim called the boy's father, who knew exactly of whom she was talking about. Although the parents insisted that they trusted their neighbor, Carissa pleaded with them to find Joe Phillips. Desperate to locate their son, they called Samuels and insisted that he check out the lead. An hour later, Joe was pulled over on the interstate with Stephen Cutler unconscious in the backseat, unharmed, for the most part. When the police inspected Joe's cabin in Wisconsin, however, they found traces of blood in his basement, and later, the skeletal remains of another missing child, buried in the backyard. When interviewed later, Carissa admitted that she hadn't witnessed Joe take Stephen with her own eyes and that it had been a premonition. Grateful for getting their son back, Stephen's parents didn't care either way, nor could they thank her enough. Detective Samuels, on the other hand, didn't like her story, but couldn't connect her in any way to the perpetrator. In the end, he thanked her for 'the hunch' and informed Carissa that she might have to testify in court. It never happened, however. Joe Phillips died of a heart attack three weeks later, in his cell.

"Wow. Thank goodness you helped save that little boy," Beth said, staring at her in wonder. "I'm just surprised Detective Samuels treated you so unfairly. I would think he'd have tried anything to find Stephen. Although," she frowned, "I told him about working with you and he wasn't exactly enthusiastic about it."

"I bet. He's a very stubborn man. He doesn't want to believe in anything that's unexplainable," said Carissa.

"But, it *is* explainable," said Beth, her eyes shining. She smiled. "You have a gift. And that's all the explaining needed."

Carissa smiled back in gratitude. "I wish everyone felt that way."

"Has it ever steered you completely wrong?" Beth asked, her smile fading.

"I've steered myself wrong by interpreting the visions incorrectly," she admitted.

"Let's hope that in the case of Mike, you have," Beth said softly.

"What about Mike?" said Tom.

They all turned to find him walking out of the hallway.

"When did you get back?" Beth asked, looking up at him.

"Just now. I let myself in through the kitchen." He looked at Carissa and Dustin. "By the way, there's plenty of food in there, if anyone's hungry. I figured you might be back."

They thanked him.

"Back to Mike. What's going on?" he asked, crossing his arms over his chest with a stoic expression on his face.

162

He would love to hear something negative about the man, Carissa thought, almost amused.

"Nothing to concern yourself with," Beth said, giving Carissa a look that warned her not to say anything.

"Is it the roads?" he asked. "They're getting pretty slippery out there. He's still heading back tonight, right?"

"Yes," said Beth. "Anyway, how about we all go into the kitchen and have a bite to eat? Meanwhile," she looked at Tom. "We can fill you in on what Carissa and Dustin learned while they were away."

"Sounds good," he replied.

Dustin patted his stomach. "To tell you the truth, we just had Taco Bell, but I'm always hungry."

"Good, because I brought back a lot of food," Tom replied. "In fact, that's why it took so long for me to get back."

"Did you get any cream cheese wontons?" Beth asked, a sad look on her face.

He nodded. "Of course." He looked at Dustin and Carissa. "They're Lainey's favorite. I figured… in case she came back tonight," he voice hitched. He looked away. "She'd be hungry."

Everyone nodded.

Chapter 31

Lainey

LAINEY AND SAMMY screamed when the masked man shot Tara and she dropped down into the snow.

"He killed her, didn't he?" sobbed Lainey from the backseat.

"Yes. I think so," Sammy answered, also shaken and crying.

The man turned away from Tara and headed back toward them.

"Oh, my God, he's going to kill us, too!" Sammy shrieked.

The killer opened up the back door and ordered Lainey to get out. Too terrified to move, Lainey curled up into a ball and wept harder.

"Lainey," the man growled angrily. "If you don't get out of this car by the time I count to five, you're going to be in seriously big trouble!"

Recognizing his voice, she looked up at him. "Why did you kill Tara, Uncle Mitch?"

Muttering to himself, he pulled his mask up, revealing his face, which was glistening with sweat. "Because she did something very bad, Lainey. Now, if you don't get out of the vehicle, I'm going to spank you so hard, you won't be able to sit for a week. Or better yet, I'm going to start shooting again and neither of us want that."

She stared at him, mouth agape.

"I mean it. Get up!" he said loudly.

164

Trembling, she obeyed. Lainey had almost believed she'd been dreaming about who'd actually kidnapped her. But witnessing this side of him, Lainey realized it really had been Mitch who'd taken her from Walmart and he was just as evil as Kurt and Yury.

"You, too!" Mitch hollered, looking over at Sammy. "Move it!"

Terrified, Sammy opened the front door and quickly got out.

Mitch pulled the mask back over his face. "Now, both of you, go and get into my truck."

"What about Tara?" Lainey already grieving for the teenager lying in the snow, blood seeping out of her thigh.

"Don't worry about her," Mitch said angrily.

Lainey's heart wrenched with sadness. She couldn't believe Tara was really gone.

Mitch's eyes dipped down at her feet. "Dammit, where are your shoes?"

Lainey was suddenly too stunned to answer him. She thought she'd seen Tara's eyes open and close.

Was she alive?

Mumbling under his breath, Mitch bent down into the backseat of the Chrysler, searching frantically for her shoes.

Tara opened up her eyes again.

Shocked and relieved, Lainey didn't say anything. She wasn't dumb. She knew if Mitch realized Tara was alive, he would probably shoot her again.

Mitch stood up straight, a frustrated look on his face. "Seriously? No shoes for either of you?"

"No," Sammy muttered. "We didn't have time to find them."

He rolled his eyes. "Of all the stupid… you'll catch pneumonia if you're not careful." He waved the gun. "Hurry up and get into the truck."

Lainey glanced back over to Tara.

What about Tara? Would she bleed to death, alone out here in the snow?
165

"Move it," snapped Mitch, trudging back to his truck.

Begrudgingly, she followed him over with Sammy.

"I still can't believe you two were wandering out here in the snow without shoes. Your toes must be freezing," Mitch said, opening up his club cab.

"Yes," they both mumbled.

He helped them into the back and gave an irritated sigh. "Take off your wet socks. I'll turn up the heat."

The children did as he ordered.

Mitch slammed the door shut and went around to the driver's side. Opening the door, he leaned in, turned the heater up, and then grabbed his cell phone from the center column.

"I'll be right back. Don't either of you dare move a muscle," he said sharply, before closing the door.

"That guy is *really* your uncle?" Sammy said, wiping the tears from his eyes.

"Not my real one. His brother is going to marry my mom," she said, watching Mitch pace back-and-forth outside.

"Why do you call him uncle?"

"He asked me to call him that, which I didn't mind before. Now, I... I hate him."

"I hate him, too," said Sammy, glaring at Mitch. "He's the guy who took me."

"Me, too," she said, watching as he began talking into his phone. "And when my mom finds out, she's going to be so angry."

"*If* she finds out," Sammy mumbled.

Lainey wondered if Mike knew about the kidnapping. Her mother would never marry him if he did. If that was the case, maybe she would even get back with her father.

"We need to try and escape again so my mom finds out about Mitch. Plus," she glanced back toward where Tara was lying, "we have to get help for Tara. She could die out here if he leaves her."

"What are you talking about? She's already dead," he said sadly.

"No. She's not. I saw her open her eyes," replied Lainey.

Relief flooded his features. "She's alive?"

Lainey nodded and smiled.

Sammy turned to look out at Tara and chewed on his lower lip. "If he realizes that she's not dead, he might shoot her again."

"I know."

A new determined look crossed his face. Sammy leaned forward and stared at the controls. "I bet I can drive this thing out of here. We could go to the police and they can call an ambulance for her."

"Do you really think you can do it?" Lainey asked, surprised.

"Yeah. I watched Tara drive the car. It didn't look so hard."

Lainey's heart began to race. "We should do it now. This is probably our last chance."

"I know." He took a deep breath. "I just hope he doesn't start shooting at us."

"Tara said we were worth a lot of money, remember? I don't think he will."

"But, you don't know for sure."

"No," she said softly.

"What's he doing now?" Sammy said, squinting toward Mitch.

Lainey looked at him. Mitch had the car's trunk open and was digging around as if looking for something.

"Keep an eye on him," Sammy said.

"Okay."

Lainey watched as Mitch walked back over to Tara and picked her up. He carried her over to the trunk of the car and set her inside. Meanwhile, Sammy quickly slid through the two front seats and settled into the driver's spot. He put one hand on the steering wheel and the other on the shifter. Releasing a shaky breath, Sammy slid the lever to the 'D' and stepped on the gas.

"You did it!" she cried as the truck began to move.

Noticing what was happening, Mitch whipped around, a shocked expression on his face. He quickly began racing toward them.

"Faster!" cried Lainey.

Sammy pressed harder on the gas and the truck sped up. The tires kicked up snow, covering Mitch as he tried catching up to them.

"You're doing it!" Lainey cried, turning her head to look out the back window. She saw Mitch fall and then get back up again, his face red with anger when he realized they were getting away.

"Yeah, but… we're going the wrong way," Sammy said glumly.

He was right. The truck was heading back toward the farm. The last place they wanted to be.

Chapter 32

Carissa

AS THEY WERE sitting down to eat, Dustin received a phone call from Jeremy. He excused himself and stepped out of the kitchen. When he returned shortly after, it was obvious he had some important news.

"What is it?" Carissa asked.

"Well, Jeremy was able to verify that Mike was indeed in Madison the last twenty-four hours. In fact, earlier today, he had lunch at a restaurant called 'Bear Creek Tavern'," Dustin said.

Tom gave him a curious look. "How did he find that out?"

"Like I said before, Jeremy worked for the government and still has connections there. I'm sure he was able to track the information by Mike's credit card usage," Dustin said.

"Makes sense. What about Friday evening when Lainey went missing?" Tom asked. "When he was supposed to be in Colorado?"

"Apparently, that checks out as well. So," he looked at Beth. "You were right about one thing. He's been exactly where he said he was."

Relieved, Beth's eyes filled with tears. She smiled. "I knew he was innocent."

Dustin stared at her for a few seconds and then sighed. "There is something else, however. We should probably talk in the other room, Beth."

She looked startled. "Something else? About Mike?"

Dustin nodded.

Beth looked at Carissa and Tom. She shrugged. "Hell, I have nothing to hide from anyone, and how bad can it be compared to everything else? Just, spit it out."

Dustin hesitated. "Jeremy actually spoke to the manager of the hotel. Apparently, he remembers Mike very well, because they struck up a conversation about art. Anyway, to make a long story short, he recalls that Mike wasn't the only one staying in his room."

"I'm sure Mitch was with him. They usually travel together," Beth said, not looking too concerned.

Dustin's eyes went to Carissa's for a brief second and then back to Beth's. "I'm sorry, Beth. The manager assumed that he was staying with his wife. That's how he introduced her, at least."

Beth's face turned red. She scowled. "*Her?*"

Dustin nodded.

"Does Mike have an assistant?" Carissa asked with a sour feeling in her stomach. "I feel like that's who this woman might be. Someone who works with him."

"Yes. Her name is Gloria. I haven't met her. She doesn't usually travel with him, though. Mitch does. I guess it's possible he took her with him this time. But, why would he tell the manager his assistant was his wife?" Beth replied, dumbfounded.

Tom let out a ragged breath. "Think about it, Beth. Why would a man feel the need to be dishonest about who he sharing his room with if he's not doing something wrong?"

She looked at him, her face stricken. "No. He wouldn't cheat on me," she said firmly. "Mike isn't like that. There has to be a logical explanation. Maybe the manager misunderstood?"

170

"I suppose it's possible. Since he'll be home soon, you can ask him about it. Just remember, the good news. He wasn't the kidnapper," Dustin replied.

"You thought he was?" Tom asked, unaware of their prior conversation.

"No. But, Carissa and Dustin thought it might be a good idea to check him out," Beth said, staring off into space.

"Good thing they did. I mean, seriously. What an asshole," said Tom, looking disgusted. "If he is cheating, which seems pretty evident, it's at the worst possible time, too."

Carissa didn't think any time was good, but she had to agree. Beth had enough on her plate and this would only make things worse. She felt horrible for her. Tom, on the other hand, was secretly elated about the news. She just knew it. He definitely wanted his wife back and this would probably make it easier for him. She still didn't know what she thought of the man, but he loved Beth and she needed someone supportive by her side. Not someone hiding secrets.

"I know this looks bad on his part, but… we're newly *engaged*. Why would Mike cheat on me? Wouldn't it be easier to just call the wedding off?" she said, her voice breaking.

Nobody said anything.

Clearly upset, Beth stood up. "I… I just can't handle this right now. I'm going to lie down. When Mike gets here, please don't say anything."

The three nodded and then watched as she left the kitchen.

"Should I go to her?" Tom asked, looking across the table at Carissa.

"Not yet," she replied, leaning back in the chair. "Let her have some time to take it all in. After she speaks to Mike, that's when she'll need you the most."

"So, you think he'll come clean?" Dustin asked.

171

"No, but something tells me things aren't going to be the same for them after this," Carissa replied softly.

Looking for Lainey   Kristen Middleton

Chapter 33

Mitch

STANDING BACK UP, Mitch brushed the snow off his jeans, shocked that the little shits had gotten away in his truck. Grabbing his phone, he called Kurt and explained what had happened.

"Wow, they're resourceful. Don't worry. I'll get 'em," Kurt replied and hung up.

Putting his phone back into his jacket, Mitch jogged back toward the farm, seeing the taillights ahead of him. He wasn't concerned about the kids getting away, he was more worried about them damaging his truck. He'd just purchased it the month before and was meticulous about all his vehicles. He already had a couple of scratches from the gravel road, which drove him nuts. Now, he'd be lucky if that's all it ended up with. Especially the way the boy was driving.

"Damn kids," he muttered.

Mitch could see Kurt approaching from the opposite direction and he slowed to a walk, watching what would happen.

Suddenly, the truck veered off the road and into the long patch of unfarmed flatland. He realized the kids were attempting to turn around and knew that if anyone else were driving, it would be doable, even in the mud. But it was obvious Sammy didn't know

173

what he was doing or how to put the truck into four-wheel drive, so they quickly became stuck.

Smiling, he watched as Kurt stopped his vehicle and got out. As he began walking through the snow toward the truck, it somehow became dislodged and within seconds, the kids appeared to be on the move once again.

Mitch stared in wonder as the truck began to circle around and head back toward him. It was obvious he'd underestimated Sammy. The eleven-year-old kid was a lot smarter than he'd anticipated.

Chapter 34

Sammy

SAMMY ALMOST PANICKED when they became stuck in the field, but then he recalled a time, last winter, when his father had driven into a blizzard. They'd been sliding all over the road until he'd put their SUV into four-wheel-drive. Immediately, the vehicle had become more manageable. Sammy had asked him about it and his dad had explained that he'd changed it from two-wheel-drive to four, because it gave the SUV more traction when needed. He remembered his father had switched something over on the dashboard. Luckily, Sammy found a knob with a two and a couple of fours. What confused him was that one four had an arrow pointing up beside it, and the other had one going down. He decided to try the one with the arrow going down, and thankfully, it worked.

Now they were on their way again and Sammy knew he had to get as far away from the kidnappers as he could, but back to the road, before they reached the woods.

"It's so bumpy!" Lainey said, as they drove through the field, both of them bouncing around in the cab.

"I know, but at least they're not coming after us."

"It looks like they're just watching," Lainey told him while looking out the back of the truck. Mitch had caught up to Kurt and both were just standing there.

175

"Maybe they know they could get stuck like we did. I don't know if they have four-wheel-drive."

"What's that?"

"Something that helps you get unstuck," he said, not really knowing why himself. He remembered his dad talking about axles and torque. The explanation had gone over his head.

"Oh."

When they finally made it back to the dirt road, Sammy noticed Kurt's car heading toward them again. With his heart hammering in his chest, he pushed harder on the gas.

"I'm scared," Lainey said, looking back.

He was frightened, too, especially with Kurt's car barreling toward them. But they weren't caught yet and he was going to try everything he could to get them out of there. Not only did Tara need their help, but there was no way he was going to let them sell him or Lainey to a bunch of pervs.

Chapter 35

Kurt

"CAN YOU BELIEVE these kids?" Kurt said angrily when Mitch got into the car.

"All I know is that if they reach the main road and someone spots them, we're finished," Mitch muttered.

"Man, Tara has never even driven a vehicle in her life but she's doing one hell of a job," Kurt continued, admiring her ingenuity. As bad as the situation was, he still couldn't help but feel proud of her. Of course, after this, Yury would probably shoot her. The thought didn't bring him any happiness or relief, however. He held a soft spot in his heart for her. Always would.

Mitch grunted. "Tara? She's not the one driving."

Kurt looked at him, surprised. "What? What do you mean?"

He shrugged. "She's dead. I had to kill her."

"Why?"

"*Why?* Because she attacked me," he snapped. "And, obviously, it needed to be done. Look at all the shit she caused us."

Kurt swallowed the lump in his throat. "So, where did you leave her?"

"Don't worry about it. I've taken care of the body."

Kurt wanted to ask him where, but they had more important things to worry about. Like the truck in front of them. He still couldn't believe that a kid was driving it.

"Anyway, this is your fault, you know. Maybe if you hadn't given her so much free reign, this might not have happened."

"No. It was Dina's fault," Kurt muttered. "She antagonized Tara so much that—"

"Oh, bullshit!" Mitch hollered. "Tara was a prisoner and you treated like a member of the family. You should have sent her away a long time ago. But you and your sick fantasies are what got us into this mess in the first place. Do you realize how close we are to getting arrested? If these kids escape, the entire operation is at risk."

"Just calm down. We'll get them," Kurt said, trying to keep his cool. Although they were childhood friends, that didn't give Mitch the right to insult him. Besides, Kurt had made him a lot of money by bringing him into the business. It had been a risky move, but Mitch had always been cold and calculating, so it had worked out. But that didn't give him the right to be an asshole.

"We'd better. Get in front of them!"

Kurt punched the accelerator down. They sped up and he maneuvered the car until they were side-by-side. He looked up and saw Lainey staring down at him, a terrified look on her face.

"Get around them!" Mitch ordered.

He tried, but then the kid accelerated and they were behind him again.

Mitch growled in irritation. Kurt obviously didn't know what the hell he was doing.

Kurt sped up again until he was next to the truck once more. This time, he jerked the steering wheel to the left, and rammed the vehicle into the truck's fender.

"What the hell?" hollered Mitch in disbelief.

178

Sammy, being inexperienced, lost control and the truck veered off the road. It spun out and flipped onto its side, the sound of crunching metal and shattering glass echoing like an explosion in the cold, dark night.

Mitch braced his hand on the glove compartment as the car fishtailed. They swerved into the ditch, and at the last minute, Kurt avoided a line of pine trees on the side of the road. When they finally came to a halt, Mitch jumped out of the car, still in shock at what had just happened. He ran over to his truck, furious that it was now a total wreck.

He's buying me a new truck, he vowed to himself angrily.

"They okay?" Kurt asked, jogging over.

Mitch peered down into the cab and saw that both kids were terrified and crying. Fortunately, the windshield and passenger side window hadn't shattered, unlike the driver's. Still, there was broken glass fragments on the flannel shirt Sammy wore. He didn't think any of them were protruding out and there didn't seem to be any blood. "Looks like it. I can't tell if they're injured, though."

"They're alive at least," Kurt said.

"Yeah. We're just lucky the airbag didn't go off," Mitch said, struggling to pull the door open. "Dammit, it's locked." He knocked on the passenger window. "Hey, unlock the door!"

Sammy stared at him with terrified eyes but didn't move.

"Unlock it!" repeated Mitch.

The boy reached over and did as he was told.

Mitch opened it and grabbed Sammy, who he noticed, despite the broken glass, had only a couple minor cuts on his left cheek. He pulled the boy out of the vehicle and handed him to Kurt, grateful he was small for his age.

"Try not to lose him again," he said sharply.

Struggling to hold Sammy, Kurt gave him a dirty look and then carried the boy back over to the car.

179

Mitch opened the back cab door and reached inside for Lainey.

"No!" she cried, crouching as far away from him as she could.

"Don't start this again," Mitch growled, his patience spent. "You kids have caused enough trouble tonight. I'm about ready to end your miserable lives. So come here or I'll shoot you like I did to Tara."

Terrified, Lainey let Mitch pull her out.

He carried her over to the car and placed her into the backseat with Sammy. When both children were safely inside, Mitch slammed the door shut and turned to face Kurt.

"You've got to be the biggest dumb-shit I've ever met in my entire life!" he yelled, unable to contain his rage any longer.

Flinching, Kurt took a step back. "What's your problem?" He waved at the car. "We got the kids back!"

Mitch grunted. "Yeah, and what about my truck, asshole?"

Kurt opened his mouth and then closed it.

"Exactly. You've got nothing to say because you're a brain-dead dipshit. I mean seriously, how am I supposed to explain this to the police?"

Kurt glanced toward the woods. "Just… just tell them something ran out in front of you. A dog or a bear or something."

Mitch laughed coldly and began to pace. "I can't be anywhere near this area with dead bodies up the road, you idiot."

"How about we just have it towed?"

He stopped walking and pointed into the distance, toward the dead farmer's place. "My vehicle is near a damn crime scene. You don't think the tow truck driver will see the news and not put two-and-two together?"

Kurt shrugged and then scratched his head. "You could always report your truck stolen."

"I guess that's what I'm going to have to do," he replied angrily and then headed back toward the truck.

180

"Whatcha doing?" Kurt called out.

"Just get in the car. I've got to make sure the kids didn't leave anything behind. Hopefully, we can get your car out of the damn ditch," he grumbled, not looking back.

"It's all wheel drive. We should be fine."

"Right," he mumbled.

Mitch stormed back over to the truck and looked inside. He couldn't believe the night he was having, and all because Kurt was a bumbling moron. As much as he enjoyed the payouts from his organization, Mitch knew it was only a matter of time before his screw-ups landed Kurt in prison. And he wasn't about to be brought down with him. It was time to cut his losses before shit really hit the fan.

Chapter 36

Carissa

IT WAS TEN-FORTY-FIVE when Beth's fiancé, Mike, walked through her front door. Carissa's first impression was that he seemed like a genuinely likeable guy.

"What's going on here?" he asked, a funny smile on his face when he noticed everyone in the living room.

Beth, who'd rejoined Dustin and Carissa, introduced them to Mike.

"Of course. So, you're the famous psychic Beth was telling me about," he said, staring at Carissa in awe. "I've always wanted to meet someone like you. I know there are a lot of fakes out there, but I hear you're the real deal."

Carissa smiled. "I have my on and off days, but would like to think I'm the 'real deal'."

He chuckled and then his face became serious. "Any new updates on Lainey?"

"No," replied Beth.

"Not enough to find her at least," Tom mumbled, from the other side of the room.

"Sorry to hear," Mike replied, putting an arm around Beth. He looked down at her. "I haven't been able to stop thinking about her myself. I feel shitty about leaving you at a time like this."

"Good thing you had someone keeping your mind off of things while you were away then," she said frostily before pulling away.

Mike gave her a confused look. "What was that?"

"We should probably head out soon so you two can catch up," Dustin said, looking uncomfortable. He stood up. "What do you say, Carissa?"

She rose from the sofa. "Yes. It's been a long day for everyone."

"And a long night for some of us, apparently," Tom said dryly.

"It was nice meeting you," Carissa said quickly, moving toward Mike. She held out her hand. "I've heard some great things about you and your work. In fact, Beth showed me the painting you did of her and Lainey. It's beautiful."

He'd painted them on the beach, making a sandcastle. The colors and details of the portrait had been quite impressive. If Mike was anything, he was talented and meticulous with his artwork.

Still looking a little perplexed, he shook her hand and thanked her.

Nothing, Carissa thought, releasing his hand. From what she could tell, Mike knew nothing about the kidnapping.

As far as the woman he'd had in his hotel room, Carissa felt as if something had happened, but knew it wasn't any of her business. Besides, she had a feeling that once the couple talked, he'd be truthful about it. He didn't seem like the kind of guy who could hold a secret like that for too long without needing to come clean. It was too bad it had to happen at such a horrible time.

"Beth, would you like me to stay?" Tom asked, shooting Mike a stern look.

She shook her head. "No. I don't think that would be a good idea. Besides, my father will be back soon."

"Okay. If you need to talk, call me," he replied, turning back to her.

"I will. Thank you," she said, looking grateful.

Tom gave her an awkward hug and then was the first out the door.

"What's wrong with him?" Mike asked, removing his jacket.

"His daughter is missing. What do you think is wrong with him?" Beth said dryly.

"Yeah, I get that," he replied, staring at her. "Have I done something wrong? Is it because I was gone?"

She sighed. "We'll talk about it."

"I'd appreciate it. I walked in here and felt like some kind of intruder," he replied.

"It's just been rough with everything going on," Carissa spoke out, trying to ease the tension in the air.

Mike relaxed. "I'm sure. Speaking of missing family members, have you spoken to my brother lately, Beth? Mitch hasn't been returning my calls and he mentioned that he was going to stop by your place this evening."

"Stop by? *Here*?" she replied, looking at him in surprise.

Mike nodded. "He didn't make it out to Madison to meet the painter yesterday."

Carissa was suddenly hit with a disturbing vision. It was enough to take her breath away.

"Excuse me, Mike? Your brother didn't fly to Denver with you last week either, did he?" she asked, the hair standing up on the back of her neck.

Mike sighed. "No. He bailed out at the last minute. Apparently, he had to meet with his financial advisor about some investments or something. Anyway, I take it you haven't heard from him, Beth?"

"No," she replied.

184

"Would you happen to have a picture of your brother?" Carissa asked, forcing a smile to her face.

His eyebrows furrowed. "Not at the moment. He's not one to stand still too long for pictures."

"I actually have one from Lainey's birthday party a few weeks back," Beth said, picking up her phone.

"Why do you want to see a picture of my brother?" Mike asked as Beth began scrolling through her photos.

"Curiosity, mostly," Carissa replied, not wanting to tell him about her suspicions. She sensed that Mike wouldn't be too impressed with her if he knew what was running through her mind.

"Here," said Beth. "I took this a couple months ago, after he gave Lainey her birthday present."

Carissa took the phone and when she saw the picture, a chill went down her spine. She looked at Beth. "There are times when I question my own intuition, wondering if I'm on the right track. This is not one of them, I'm afraid."

"What are you saying?" Beth asked, alarmed.

Carissa took a deep breath, knowing what she was about to say would cause an uproar. "I wasn't sure before about the others. Not one-hundred percent. But this time, I'd bet money on it. Mitch is the one who took Lainey from Walmart."

Chapter 37

Tara

AFTER GETTING LOCKED inside the trunk, Tara found herself in-and-out of consciousness. Shivering and in pain, she was too frightened to call out for help, thinking that the guy who shot her would come back and finish her off.

"Tara!" hollered a voice, rousing her back from the darkness. *Kurt.*

Opening her eyes, she called out to him, uncertain of the fate that awaited her once he opened the trunk. But his voice sounded desperate, and as much as she hated the man, Tara didn't think he was there to kill her.

"Hold on. I'll get you out," he promised.

Trembling, she closed her eyes and was drifting off again when she heard Kurt arguing with someone. She immediately recognized the other voice as the man who'd shot her.

"We have to get her out of there," Kurt said angrily.

Her heart sunk.

"No. She stays," replied the other man firmly.

"Are you crazy? She'll bleed to death. You shot her in the thigh, for God's sake. That's got to hurt like hell. I thought you said you killed her."

"Actually, I kind of thought she'd be dead by now," he said, a smile in his voice.

"What in the hell has gotten into you?" Kurt snapped.

"I'm coming to my senses. Which is more than I can say about you."

"What is that supposed to mean?"

"We're screwed. Yury is going to cut his losses and move the entire operation."

"Of course. He already mentioned that. We're moving," Kurt said, sounding haggard.

"Not we. *Him*. He's going to want to get rid of loose ends and disappear. Without you or me."

"Why would he do that?"

"Because he's Russian mafia. They don't have time for mistakes like this. He's probably already planning our funerals as we speak."

"You're being paranoid."

The other man grunted. "This is why you're more of a liability than an advantage. Sorry, man,"

Kurt gasped. "Wait a second. What are you doing?"

"It's better this way. At least for me."

A gun went off and Tara heard a loud thud. Shocked, she closed her eyes and became very still.

A few seconds later, the trunk opened up and the shooter placed Kurt's body inside with her.

"I know you're alive," he said, a smile in his voice.

Tara opened up her eyes and stared at the masked man.

"You don't have long, though," he said, glancing down at her thigh. "Maybe I should finish you off. Put you out of your misery."

187

"Please," she begged, her eyes filling with tears. "Don't kill me."

He stared at her for a few seconds and then slammed the trunk shut.

Chapter 38

Carissa

AS EXPECTED, MIKE protested the idea of his brother being involved.

"You're a nutcase," he said angrily. "Accusing my brother of something like that? Beth," he turned to her, "you know Mitch. He isn't a pedophile and he certainly would never harm Lainey."

Beth nodded.

"I think you should leave," he said, scowling at Carissa.

"Now hold on," Dustin said evenly. "Let's hear her out—"

"Hear her out? She just accused my brother of kidnapping Beth's daughter! This is insane!" Mike began to pace. "My brother was right about psychics. They're all lying wackos out to make a buck."

"He's right. Mitch is such a nice guy and would never do something like this," Beth said, looking uncomfortable.

"I need a drink," Mike said, heading toward the kitchen. He looked back over his shoulder. "And they need to leave."

Beth didn't reply.

He disappeared into the other room.

"I'm sorry," Carissa said softly. "I know it might sound insane, but think about this… Lainey allowed the kidnapper to get close to her at Walmart. Close enough for him to reach over and touch her face. Most kids would back away from someone they didn't know. And now we've learned that he was in town when she disappeared."

"Okay, fine. That's something to think about. But he's such a sweet guy. He loves Lainey," Beth said shakily. "I can't imagine him being involved with something like this."

"Listen," Dustin said in a low voice, "I understand how difficult this must be for you, but if Carissa strongly believes he might be involved, it's definitely worth checking out."

Beth let out a ragged sigh and then nodded.

Carissa touched her arm. "I'm sorry, Beth. Sometimes the ones closest to us are hiding the most secrets. Yes, there is a chance I'm wrong, but," she licked her lips, "I have never felt so strongly about a suspect before."

Her eyes filled with tears. "What can I do to help?"

"Do you have an address for him?" Dustin asked.

"He lives in Stillwater, right off of the St. Croix River. On Acorn Path. I don't have a house number for you. I forgot," she replied softly.

"Don't worry. We'll get it. What's his last name?" Dustin asked, uncapping his pen.

"Olson," she said.

He wrote it down and shoved the notepad back into his pocket. "We'll do some checking around and call you later, okay?"

She nodded.

Carissa reached over and gave Beth a hug. "I'm sorry. I just want to help you find her."

"I know," she said in a sad voice.

As Carissa stepped back, Mike entered the room again, holding a beer. He didn't say anything, just crossed his arms over his chest with a brooding look on his face.

"Goodnight," Dustin said, walking toward the front door.

"Goodnight," Beth replied.

Carissa followed him out.

Chapter 39

Mitch

AS MITCH WALKED away from Tara, he wondered if he was making a mistake by not putting a bullet into her head. Admittedly, killing Kurt had given him a small thrill, but, something had come over him when he'd stared into the teen's face. He didn't know if it was guilt or compassion. Those things were normally foreign to him.

Whatever the case was, he had more important things to attend to. Besides, Tara hadn't seen his face and couldn't identify him. They'd never even met face-to-face.

Mitch got into the car and removed the ski mask. Then he began driving back toward the farmhouse to find Yury. As he ran a hand through his hair, he could hear Lainey and Sammy sniveling.

"Hey. Quit your crying. You know, it's both of your faults that Tara is dead," Mitch lied, looking at them in the rearview mirror. Making them believe she was dead could only give him leverage. "Now, if you two want to stay alive, you'd better behave and not try any more shit."

Neither replied.

Mitch pulled up to the house right as Yury was stuffing a large, black duffel bag into the trunk of his rental. He took the keys out

192

of the ignition and looked back over his shoulder. "Stay here," he ordered.

They both stared at him with wide, red-rimmed eyes.

Mitch got out of the car.

"What in the hell happened out there?" Yury asked, walking over to him.

"The kids flipped my truck and Kurt is dead," Mitch said, keeping his hand on the gun hidden inside of his jacket pocket.

Yury's eyes widened in surprise. "What? *How*?"

"It was an accident," he lied. "Look, I've got the kids and want to get the hell out of here before the shit really hits the fan. I'm going to need my cut of the money now. Considering that this is the second time I've brought the little shits to you, and my truck is destroyed, I think I deserve a bonus, too."

Yury's face darkened. "You don't get paid the rest of the money until we do."

"Sorry, pal. You're going to have to make an exception this time. I just saved your ass and returned the kids," he replied with a cold smile. "I certainly didn't do it for free."

"I don't have that kind of cash sitting around," Yury said angrily. "Besides, you don't make the demands. I'm the one in charge here—"

Mitch pulled out his gun. "Not right now. Look, I'm not an idiot. I know you're going to skip town and I'm going to be left high-and-dry. Either you pay me right this minute, or you won't see these kids again."

Swearing, Yury glared at him. "You have no idea who you're threatening. You pull that trigger and my associates will hunt you down—and believe me, they *will* find you. And when they do, you, along with everyone you love, will suffer unimaginably. So, you'd better rethink your approach."

Mitch grunted. He'd heard Yury use the same lines before. "I just handed over my brother's future step-kid. Do you think I scare easily or care what happens to family?"

"No, but I imagine you care about your intestines, which will be fed to the pigs up the road if you keep this up."

Mitch chuckled. The man had a gun trained on him and was still making threats. "Come on, Yury. You must have *some* cash on you."

The two men stared at each other for several seconds and then Yury let out a ragged sigh. "Okay. Okay. I guess I understand where you're coming from. And, you're right. We'll be leaving town. Let me get my duffel bag," he said, walking back toward the trunk of his car. "I will give you what I can for your services."

Mitch followed him, prepared for anything.

"You know, even though you are an asshole, I admire you," Yury said, unzipping the duffel bag. "Your friend Kurt told me you were a shrewd businessman. I see that he was right."

Mitch remained silent, keeping his eye closely on Yury's back. "My services aren't free. If that's being shrewd, then so be it."

The front door of the farmhouse opened and Dina stepped outside with two suitcases. When she noticed Mitch holding the gun, she froze.

"What's going on?" she asked, her eyes wide with fright.

"Nothing I can't handle," Yury said before twisting around with a pistol of his own.

Mitch, not particularly surprised, fired his gun. The bullet hit Yury in the chest and he toppled to the ground

Dina gasped and dropped the suitcases.

Mitch turned toward her.

"Please, don't kill me," she begged, crying. "I won't say anything."

"I know," he replied, walking toward the porch.

194

Her eyes widened as he raised the gun.

"Sorry. You've seen my face," he said.

"Wait. I—"

Mitch pulled the trigger and watched in satisfaction as the bullet hit her in the forehead, causing dark blood and brain matter to splatter everywhere. He shoved the gun into his jacket and walked back over to Yury. Mitch searched his duffel bag and found nothing but a few articles of clothing and a laptop.

"Dammit," he grumbled.

He pulled out Yury's wallet and found a small amount of cash along with a couple of credit cards. Pocketing the money, he tossed the wallet into the trunk and decided to put Yury there, too, along with Dina. Unfortunately, the task proved to be more difficult than he'd anticipated, especially with the Russian's massive weight.

Suddenly, his phone rang. Noticing that it was his brother, he answered it.

"What's up, Mike?"

"Hey man. Sorry to bother you so late."

"No problem," he replied, trying to sound as natural as possible. "How was the trip to Madison?"

"It went well. Anyway, that's not why I'm calling." Mike then went on to tell him about meeting the psychic, Carissa Jones, and how she suspected Mitch of being Lainey's kidnapper."

Mitch's mouth went dry. "You're kidding?" he replied. "*Me?*"

"I know, right? Anyway, I just wanted to give you a heads-up, in case the police show up and start asking questions."

Mitch swore inwardly. "You know I'm not involved."

"Of course I know you're not," Mike said angrily. "She's a fraud and a nutcase."

"Exactly," he said, pacing back and forth. "They all are."

"I read about some of the other cases she helped solve, but obviously she's just been lucky. I mean, to accuse you, of all people. The woman is a head-case."

"No shit. What did Beth say about it?"

"Not much. I think she's disappointed that this woman made such an outlandish accusation."

As much as Mitch enjoyed the rush of walking on the edge, he felt as if he was beginning to teeter the wrong way. Especially after the last hour.

"So, do you think Carissa is going to go to the cops with this?" he asked, trying to remain calm.

"I don't know. Hell, who cares if she does? It's obviously bullshit; nobody is going to believe you'd be in on something like that. Anyway, I have to go. Beth seems to think that Gloria and I are having an affair."

He snorted. "Did the psychic tell her this, too?"

"No. apparently, the hotel manager told her that we'd shared a room together."

He raised his eyebrows. "You did?"

"Yeah, but not for that reason. I was just trying to save money," he replied defensively. "The hotel room was four-hundred a night and there were two beds in my room."

"So, you two didn't fool around?"

He let out a weary sigh and lowered his voice. "Things may have happened, but, it didn't mean anything. It was definitely a one-time deal."

His little brother's mishap was nothing compared to what he'd been going through that evening. "You're going to have to fire her."

"Nah. We both agreed it shouldn't have ever happened. Gloria felt guilty about it, too. It will be fine."

"You telling Beth the truth?"

"She has nothing to worry about," he said firmly. "That's the truth and that's what I told her."

He had heard this before. His brother was relatively a good man, but he had a weakness: Women. That's why none of his relationships lasted. He couldn't stay monogamous for too long, which was why it had surprised him when Mike had gotten engaged.

"Beth's dad just arrived. I've gotta go."

"Well, thanks for the heads-up," said Mitch.

"No problem."

Mitch hung up and quickly returned to the task of fitting the two dead bodies into the trunk. Afterward, he walked back over to the porch and kicked some snow over the bloodstains. Realizing he had to do better than that, he pulled a large, empty planter over the remaining evidence and then headed back to the car, his mind reeling on what to do about the kids. He knew he couldn't let them go, and killing the children seemed like a waste, so he made a decision: he would sell the little shits himself. Kurt had mentioned how and where to find buyers. Ones that would pay top dollar if the merchandise was worth it. The problem was that they wouldn't make a deal with a stranger. Only someone trustworthy, like Yury, who he knew went by the name 'Cobra' on the dark web. Cobra had a reputation and a large clientele of pervs. At least that's what Kurt had told him.

Mitch glanced back over at Yury's rental car and an idea began to take shape. One that could solve a lot of problems.

If Cobra's clients thought they were dealing with Cobra, they'd strike a deal.

He walked back to the trunk and opened it. Mitch grabbed the laptop, along with the man's ID, and locked it back up. He knew that in time, someone would find the dead bodies, but, if he played his cards right, they wouldn't ever connect him.

197

"Where are we going?" Sammy asked as they drove away from the farmhouse.

Mitch knew it was risky, but he had no other choice than to bring them back to his place until he could figure out what to do from there. As for the psychic, he knew there wasn't anything she could do. Even if she went to the police, all they'd do is question him. And, if he needed an alibi, he'd find one.

"Don't worry about it," he said, scowling at the boy in the rearview mirror.

Sammy sank farther into the seat and looked away.

Chapter 40

Carissa

"YOU REALLY THINK Mike's brother is involved, huh?" Dustin asked as he started the engine.

"Yes."

Dustin nodded toward the clock. "I know it's late, but… the clock is ticking for Lainey. Should we head out to Stillwater and check him out?"

"I think it's a good idea," she replied.

"I'll call Jeremy again. Hopefully he isn't asleep yet."

She nodded and stared out into the darkness as Dustin made the call. As close as they were to finding Lainey, Carissa felt like they still had a long way to go.

MITCH LIVED IN a newly built, two-story home right off the St. Croix River. It was surrounded by trees and very private, much like most of the other homes in that particular area.

As they drove up the snow-covered driveway, Dustin whistled. "This place must have cost a bundle, especially being right on the river."

"Crime pays well," she said dryly.

"That, and I'm sure he makes a lot with the art gallery," replied Dustin.

They'd learned that Mitch also owned the fifty acres of land that surrounded his home, which he'd purchased two years ago, along with a couple of other vacant lots further north.

"He must be sleeping," Dustin said, as they stared at the dark house.

"I don't think he's home," she replied. "There weren't any tire tracks leading to the garage, and nobody has shoveled yet."

"Good point," he said.

She sighed.

"What should we do? Wait around until he gets back and try talking to him?"

They'd already discussed how they'd handle the conversation. Dustin would explain that he was working with Beth's father and wanted to interview everyone who knew Lainey. Of course, it would seem strange for them to be there at such a late hour. But every minute counted and there was no other way around it, which couldn't be argued. They also knew there was always the chance that Mike would call his brother and tell him about the crazy psychic who was accusing him of kidnapping.

"Yeah, we should wait, at least for a while. In the meantime, I'm going to get out and walk around the place. See if I can pick something up."

"Okay," he said, shutting off the engine.

Carissa got out and began walking toward the house. Although it was dark, there were yard lights that lit up the property, making it easier to see. When she reached the backyard, she saw that it sloped down to the river, where there was a small boathouse and a dock.

"He has a home security installed, so be careful," Dustin said, startling her.

She turned and nodded toward the house. "It looks like he has blinds on every window, too, so we couldn't see much inside anyway."

"Do you think Lainey might be in there somewhere?" Dustin asked, studying the place.

"No. I don't think so," she replied. "But, I feel like we could find some answers here. I also sense… danger."

"I do, too," he said. "Although, I'm sure it's because we're sneaking around someone's house in the middle of the night. That's always dangerous."

She smiled. "True."

"Hell, we don't even know if he's returning tonight," he said, stuffing his hands into his pockets. "We could be wasting our time here. Maybe we should just return in the morning?"

Carissa sighed. She could see that he was exhausted, and it had been a long day. Plus, he was right. For all they knew, Mitch was out and about, abducting more children.

"Let's just wait around until twelve-thirty and leave if he doesn't show."

He nodded.

"We're coming back tomorrow, though," she said, brushing the windblown hair out of her face. "He's in on it. I just know it."

AT TWELVE-THIRTY, THEY gave up and drove back to the restaurant where Carissa had left her SUV several hours earlier.

"You sure you don't want to crash at my place?" Dustin asked with a devilish grin. "I'll even sleep on the sofa."

"You forget who you're talking to," she replied, smiling back. "I can read your mind."

He chuckled. "Maybe I want you to," he said, leaning closer. "You have no idea how much I've missed you."

"I've missed you, too," she replied softly.

"Then come home with me."

"You know I can't. As much as I'd like to, I need to stay focused on this case and keep my mind clear."

He sighed. "I know. When this is over, though, no excuses."

"No excuses."

He nodded toward her vehicle, which was covered in snow. "Would you like help with that?"

"Nah. I'll be fine."

"Okay. Call me as soon as you get home. So I know you made it safely."

"I will."

He pulled her to him and they kissed each other goodbye.

"Drive safely," she said, getting out of the truck.

"You, too."

Carissa walked to her SUV. She got inside and turned on her windshield wipers while Dustin patiently waited for her. Waving, she drove out of the parking lot and headed home.

Chapter 41

Mitch

WHEN MITCH PULLED into his driveway, he noticed a fresh set of tire tracks in the snow and his stomach tightened. Someone had been at his place and very recently.

The psychic?

It seemed logical, especially after the conversation he'd just had with Mike. Seething at the idea, he tapped his fingers on the steering wheel. He wasn't sure, but knew she had to be dealt with. And soon.

Turning the house alarm off from his phone app, he pulled into the garage and quickly shut the door.

Mitch looked back at the children. "Out," he ordered.

They silently obeyed.

Mitch brought Lainey and Sammy into the house and checked their feet. Relieved that neither child had gotten frostbite, he gave them each a pair of dry wool socks.

"Are you going to sell us?" Sammy asked nervously as he pulled the oversized socks over his feet.

Mitch had been thinking things over on the way back to his place and had decided that telling them the truth wouldn't help the situation. They'd try to escape again, and he didn't have time to go chasing them around again. Plus, he had neighbors up the road,

203

and the last thing he needed was to draw their attention. "Sell you? Nah. In fact, if you listen to me and don't pull any funny business, I was thinking I might bring you back to your parents," he lied.

"Really?" said Sammy, looking surprised.

"Yeah. The truth is, I didn't know they were going to try and sell you kids," he continued.

"Why did you kidnap us then?" Sammy asked, his eyes narrowing.

As annoying as the boy was, Mitch was impressed with his courage. Especially after everything he'd witnessed. Instead of clamming up in fear, Sammy was demanding answers from a kidnapper.

"They were framing me and I had no choice," he replied.

"For what?" he asked.

"Something that you're better off not knowing. They're gone now, though, and no longer a threat, which means I can do whatever I want with you two. I can even bring you home." He stared at both of them hard. "But, only if you do what I say."

Sammy relaxed a little. "Okay."

Lainey, on the other hand, looked at him suspiciously. "Why did you kill Tara?"

"She was one of them," Mitch said.

"No, she wasn't," Lainey replied, her eyes filling with tears. "She helped us escape and… you *shot* her."

"We all make mistakes," he mumbled, tired of the questions, the whining, and the crying. "I guess I did, too, by kidnapping you."

Sammy and Lainey stared at him, obviously still not sure what to think.

"Seriously, kid, I'm sorry I shot your friend. If it makes you feel better, I didn't kill her. I'm sure the cops will be showing up any minute and they'll rescue her."

"Can't you call an ambulance for her?" Lainey asked quickly.

He forced a smile to his face. "Sure. Why not? But only if you promise to get some sleep. Okay?"

Lainey nodded.

Mitch sighed in relief.

"Can't you just bring us home now?" Sammy asked.

Mitch's eye twitched.

Give them an inch and they ask for a mile.

He seriously needed a drink.

"It's in the middle of the night and your parents are sleeping. Behave and you'll see them tomorrow. Understand?" he said.

They both nodded.

"Good," he replied. "Now, let's go."

Mitch brought them downstairs to the large wine cellar, which was still a work-in-progress. It was the only place in the house without windows and it also had a door, one that didn't lock, but he planned on changing that promptly.

"We have to sleep in *here*?" Sammy said when Mitch turned on the light.

He looked around the bare, cedar-lined room. As far as he was concerned, it was better than the ratty, old farmhouse they'd been staying in. And it smelled of fresh wood instead of the dank, musty scent that permeated through the old house.

"Come on now. It could be much worse. I do have an air mattress you both can share," he replied. "I'm going to bring you some warm milk to drink as well. It will help you sleep."

"Warm milk?" repeated Sammy, grimacing. "I don't even like cold milk."

"You'll like this. I promise you. Stay here and sit down. I'll be back," Mitch said before heading back upstairs.

When he reached the kitchen, Mitch took some milk out of the refrigerator, along with two mugs from the cupboard, and poured a

205

little into each mug. He followed it up with a small pad of butter and some sugar, like his mother used to when he and Mike were kids. Then, he put the mugs into the microwave. As they warmed up, he went to the master bathroom and grabbed a bottle of Nyquil, something he knew would help the kids sleep. Once everything was ready, he went back downstairs and offered each of the children a mug.

"I tried making it warm and not too hot," he said, watching as they stared down into their mugs curiously. "By the way, I want each of you to take some of this." He pulled out the bottle of Nyquil from his jacket pocket.

"I'm not sick," Sammy said, looking confused.

"Maybe not, but it will help you sleep," Mitch said, pouring a capful of it. He handed it to the boy. "I know it doesn't taste the greatest, so drink it down quickly and chase it with the warm milk."

Sammy frowned.

"Do it," Mitch said sternly.

Licking his lips, the boy forced the liquid down his throat and shuddered.

"Drink some of the milk now," he said to him, taking back the cap.

Sammy brought the mug to his lips and took a sip. "Yuck," he mumbled.

Ignoring him, Mitch poured another capful of Nyquil and handed it to Lainey. She drank it down and also made a face.

He took the cap from her and then went in search of the air mattress. Once everything was set up, he made each of them use the bathroom.

"I should warn you, I have an alarm on the house and booby-traps hidden all around the yard. The kind that will blow your face right off of your skull," he lied. "Only I know where they are, and if you were to try and leave, you'll die."

The children stared at him with wide eyes.

"Now, get some sleep and we'll talk about returning you to your parents tomorrow," he said.

They both nodded.

"I'm going back upstairs to arm the house and get some sleep myself. Like I said, don't open any doors or try to leave. You'll end up all over my lawn. Got it?"

They both nodded again.

Satisfied that the children were too frightened to leave the house, he headed upstairs and snorted a line of coke, knowing his night was far from over. Afterward, he slipped back into the garage and slid into Kurt's car, which needed to disappear. As he opened up the garage, his thoughts went back to the kids.

What if they didn't believe his story and tried to escape?

They certainly weren't locked inside, and in fact, could potentially walk out the front door while he was away.

Rubbing his nose, he told himself it was just the coke making him paranoid; after the story he'd told them about the booby-traps, Sammy and Lainey weren't going anywhere.

Mitch started the engine and drove the vehicle to a twenty-four-hour supermarket, ten miles from his house. After parking in the back, he wiped the car clean of fingerprints and then called himself a cab. As he waited for the taxi, he decided to report his truck stolen later in the morning, around the time he normally left for work. That would seem less suspicious.

Forty-five minutes later, he was back at home and logging into the dark web, using Yury's computer.

Chapter 42

Carissa

ALTHOUGH SHE WAS exhausted, Carissa lay in bed, staring up at the ceiling. She'd tried meditating earlier, to see if any new visions would come to her, but she couldn't seem to relax enough to clear her mind. All she could think about was Mike's brother, Mitch. She felt compelled to drive back to Stillwater and set up her own surveillance. Although, she didn't know if he was returning for the night, or even truly believed he had Lainey at his place, the urgency to return there was driving her nuts.

Maybe I should call Detective Samuels?

Right.

He would probably hang up on her again. Samuels was stubborn about his beliefs and would never acknowledge her gifts.

Pushing the blankets off of her, Carissa got out of bed and went to the kitchen to make herself a cup of chamomile tea. As she opened up the cupboard, an image of a young woman came to her. Carissa thought she looked as if she were trapped somewhere and trying to get out. The vision was so intense, Carissa knew it had to be real.

Quickly, she sat down in the middle of the kitchen floor and closed her eyes. Taking deep belly breaths, she inhaled and then exhaled several times, until she felt calm and steady. Carissa then

208

pictured a door opening in her mind, allowing any further intuitive messages from beyond to be received. After a couple of minutes, she saw a car in a ditch. It was in a rural area, without a lot of traffic or houses nearby. She waited patiently until another image flashed into her head. This time, it was Lainey and a boy; they were in an empty room, one that was filled with dozens of wine racks. A man was in the room with them, filling up an air mattress.

Mitch?

Her gut told her it was.

The last vision she had was of socks again.

What was with the socks?

Carissa opened her eyes. She got up off the floor and grabbed her cell phone. She called Dustin and he answered on the third ring.

"What's up?" he murmured.

"Mitch has the kids at his place," she said quickly.

"What? We were just there. Are you sure?"

She explained her vision. "Okay, so maybe I don't know for sure, but it feels right to me."

"That's good enough for me," he said, now sounding wide awake.

His confidence in her abilities made her warm inside. "I'm coming with you."

"No. It's too dangerous."

"Dustin, if you think I'm letting you confront Mitch alone, you've got another thing coming."

"I won't go alone. I'll call the police if that makes you feel better."

Carissa relaxed. Still, she wanted to be there and told him.

"No," he argued. "If something goes wrong, I don't want you hurt. I'll call Detective Samuels."

"What are you going to tell him?"

"I don't know yet. Let me worry about that. You just stay put. Understand?"

"Yes," she mumbled.

"I'll call you when I know something."

"Okay."

Chapter 43

Dustin

AFTER HANGING UP with Carissa, Dustin looked up Detective Samuels' phone number and left him a message. They'd spoken together on a few occasions and, in fact, the two had once worked at the same precinct. The man was definitely a hard-head, and Dustin knew convincing him to check out Mitch would be almost improbable. Especially when he told him why he believed that Mitch was now a suspect.

A short time later, Dustin was in his truck and heading back toward Mitch's place. As he drove onto the freeway, his phone rang. It was Samuels.

"So, what proof do you have that this guy, Mitch, is involved with the kidnapping?" Samuels asked him.

Dustin took a deep breath and told him the truth. It was truly all he had and something told him he'd find out about Carissa's allegation from Beth anyway.

"You're assuming he's involved because Carissa Jones saw it in a 'vision'?" he replied wryly.

"It's a good lead, and you know damn good and well that she's helped with cases similar to this before. Like the one you were involved with last year," he reminded him.

Samuels grunted. "She was lucky."

211

It was like pulling teeth with him, thought Dustin.

"Luck? She didn't even know the kidnapper but ID'd him and saved that little boy. Anyway, the point is that everyone around Lainey should be a suspect, especially since the video shows how she responded to the kidnapper. You saw it. Lainey *knew* the man who took her. It was on her face."

"Have you talked to Beth about this guy yet?"

"Yes and, to be honest, she wasn't sure what to think." Dustin then told him about Mitch being in town the night Lainey was taken. "He was supposed to be in Colorado with his brother, Mike, but stayed behind."

Samuels let out a ragged breath. "Look, we'll go and interview him tomorrow. Not in the middle of the night."

"And what if it's too late? What if he has her right now and tomorrow, Lainey is out of our reach?"

"I highly doubt her future brother-in-law, Mitch, has her locked away in his cellar. Hell, even if he is involved, which is highly unlikely, he isn't going to let us in anyway, and we don't have a search warrant. Now, I know you're just trying to help, but the hell if I'm going on some kind of wild goose chase, especially at this hour. Especially because of some psychic's *hunch*."

Dustin knew the conversation wasn't going anywhere and he was on his own. "Fine. You interview him tomorrow," he said evenly. "And while you're doing it, you might want to check out his financial situation. He's obviously pulling in a lot of cash. More than someone who's a co-owner of a modest art gallery."

"From what Beth said, the two brothers seem to be doing very well for themselves in the art business," Samuels said.

"Maybe. Maybe not. I'd still check it out," Dustin replied, thinking of Mitch's home. "I would think that a newly constructed place like that, right on the river, had to cost well over a million dollars. I also heard he owns over fifty acres of land."

212

"We'll look into it."

"Thank you."

"Now, is there anything else Ms. Jones is predicting that I should be concerned about?" he asked dryly. "Maybe a shooting in Minneapolis, or a drug deal gone wrong in St. Paul? Or are her premonitions strictly limited to missing children in the suburbs?"

Dustin rolled his eyes. He hadn't changed a bit. "Carissa is passionate about helping children, so I imagine that's why she focuses on that more than anything. Anyway, I just want you to take this lead seriously. It could save Lainey."

"I'll do what I can."

After hanging up, Dustin continued his route to Stillwater, deciding not to tell Carissa that he was going to Mitch's alone. She wouldn't stand for it, and more than likely, get in her SUV and meet him there.

Chapter 44

Mitch

MITCH SPENT THE next hour trying to figure out how Yury ran his auctions on the dark web, and found it was more difficult to maneuver around than he'd anticipated. One couldn't just look up 'how to sell children' and be provided with trusted instructions and links. And then there was the possibility of causing red flags, especially since he didn't know what he was doing. Of course, from what Kurt had explained before, the Tor program was supposed to help hide his true I.P. address. Still, it was all new to him, and he knew one wrong move could jeopardize everything.

After about an hour into his search, Mitch stumbled upon a site he found in Yury's browsing history, where he was automatically logged in. Or, at least "Cobra" was. It was there he clicked into a chatroom and was quickly greeted by someone named "Johnnyrotpotato." Immediately, this person sent him a private message, asking about the auction.

Mitch grinned. "Bingo."

Johnnyrotpotato: *I saw the pix of the newest merchandise. Very impressive. The sale is Friday at 7pm still, correct?*

Mitch wanted to ask him where he'd seen the photos, but refrained. He imagined Yury uploaded them into his own part of the dark web to build hype up for the upcoming auction.

Cobra: *Not sure. Having some issues and might just sell the merchandise earlier.*

Johnnyrotpotato: *Issues? What kind?*

Cobra: *They're personal. I can't get into it.*

Johnnyrotpotato: *So, what's the bottom price you'd be asking?*

Mitch felt his heart begin to race. Maybe he could get rid of the kids sooner than he'd thought. He decided to request a price that sounded reasonable, although he had no idea if he was low-balling the asking amount.

Cobra: *$100,000 for both.*

There was a long pause and then:

Johnnyrotpotato: *How about $50k for both?*

Mitch frowned. Obviously, he would take it, but wasn't about to give up that easily.

Cobra: *Sorry. $100k for both. You know of anyone serious about buying, let me know.*

Mitch could tell he was typing something, and waited.

215

Johnnyrotpotato: *Okay. $75k for both. My final offer.*

He tapped his thumb nervously, unsure of what to do. The money sounded good, and he knew he had to lose the kids as soon as possible. But, he didn't know who the hell this 'Johnny' person really was.

He could even be a cop.

Paranoid, Mitch started typing his refusal when the magic words popped up on his screen. Ones that changed his mind.

Johnnyrotpotato: *I'll even pay mileage and shipping fees. Like last time.*

Mitch smiled in relief. This guy had done business with Yury before. That was all he needed to know.

Cobra: *Accepted. $75k. For both.*

Johnnyrotpotato: *Great. I'll send you an address and will wire you half now and half upon receipt of said merchandise. Just like last time.*

Cobra: *Sounds good.*

Johnnyrotpotato: *Obviously, discretion and trust needs to go both ways. I will not tolerate anything less. Nor will my associates.*

Mitch wasn't sure of which associates he was referring to, but he had no intention of screwing over the buyer. He would even personally deliver the little shits himself.

Cobra: *Understandable.*

After they discussed where to wire the money, 'Johnny' requested a dated video for proof of 'merchandise'. Mitch agreed, and after a few more seconds of chatting, the two logged off.

Mitch shut down the laptop and picked up his phone. He turned off the lights and was about to leave his office when he looked out the window and noticed a pair of headlights in the far distance.

Chapter 45

Dustin

DUSTIN DROVE SLOWLY toward Mitch's place. As he drew closer to the winding driveway, he turned off his lights. The house looked quiet, but from the extra tire tracks in the snow, he suspected the man was now home.

Shutting off the engine, he took a look through his binoculars to get a closer view of the place. It was then that his phone rang.

Carissa.

Sighing, he answered it.

"What's happening?" she asked in a shaky voice.

"Nothing. I just arrived back at Mitch's."

"Is Samuels with you?"

"No."

She sucked in her breath. "You're by yourself?"

"Yes. I'm fine, though. Don't worry."

"What did Samuels say?"

"Not much. I don't think he believes Mitch had anything to do with the case."

"So, he's not checking him out?" she asked in disbelief.

"He is. But not until later in the day."

She groaned. "Let me guess, he found out that I'm involved?"

218

"I had to tell him the truth. I'm sure he'll speak to Beth and she'll inform him of how you initially alleged Mitch's involvement earlier."

Carissa was silent for a few seconds and then sighed. "I suppose. What about Dubov?"

"His partner? What about her?"

"I've met her before. She's not as pig-headed as Samuels and might take me more seriously."

"Do you have her number?"

"Yeah. She gave me her card during the Stephen Cutler kidnapping. Unlike Samuels, she didn't treat me like a total flake."

"I suppose it wouldn't hurt to call her," Dustin said, lifting his binoculars again.

Had he seen movement by the house?

"I think it's worth a shot and we're running out of time." She sighed. "What are you planning on doing, now that you're there?"

"I'm going to try and get close to the house again. I think he's home now, too."

She groaned. "Crap. That figures. And you're alone. You be careful."

"I'll be fine."

"Dustin, I'm getting some bad vibes about this," she replied.

"Don't worry about me. This isn't my first surveillance, you know," he said with a wry smile.

"I know, but… I'm just worried."

"Your lack of confidence in my P.I. skills is a little disheartening, my dear," he teased.

"You know that's not true. I'm just worried. You can never be too cautious, you know?"

"Carissa, get some sleep," Dustin repeated. "If something comes up, I'll call you."

She let out a ragged sigh. "Okay."

"I love you."

"I love you, too."

He hung up and was about to raise the binoculars again, when someone rapped on the driver's side window. Startled, Dustin turned to find their suspect, Mitch Olson, staring at him, a furious look on his face.

Shit.

He rolled down his window.

"Are you lost?" Mitch asked coldly.

Dustin forced a smile to his face. "Sorry. I live up the street and lost my dog. I thought I saw him heading over here."

Mitch studied his face. "I haven't seen him. This is private property. You shouldn't be here."

"Aren't you going to ask what kind of dog I have?"

"I don't care. I didn't see yours or anyone else's dog on my property. Which is probably a good thing for you."

What an asshole, thought Dustin.

"Sorry. I'll be on my way."

Glaring at him, Mitch stepped backward and folded his arms across his chest. It was at that moment Dustin noticed something on the man's elbow. Grabbing his phone, he turned on the flashlight and aimed it toward the man's ski jacket.

"What the hell?" growled Mitch, shielding his eyes from the light.

"Sorry, I thought I saw my dog behind you," he replied. The stain on his elbow definitely looked like blood. "I'll be on my way now."

Frowning, Mitch looked over his shoulder.

Dustin rolled his window up quickly and started the engine.

Could it have been Lainey's blood?

Heart pounding, he backed his vehicle away from the house until he was back on the road. From there, he drove a couple

220

blocks away and parked on a dark street. After waiting around for a time, he got out and crept back to the house.

Chapter 46

Mitch

MITCH WASN'T STUPID. He knew the stranger probably didn't even own a dog and was stalking him. He also had a feeling he was there because of the psychic.

I should leave with the kids.

But where could he go?

He couldn't rent a motel room. There were bulletins everywhere showing the children's faces. Mitch's only choice was to play it cool and stay put. Obviously, his brother and Beth didn't think he was involved with the kidnapping and there wasn't any real evidence connecting him to it. At least he didn't think he'd left anything behind in his truck. Plus, the police couldn't search his house without a warrant and he knew a judge would hardly grant one *just* because some psychic was trying to incriminate him. All Mitch needed to do was relax and things would work themselves out.

Still, he had a feeling the trespasser would be back, and that didn't sit well with him.

After doing another line of coke, Mitch grabbed a set of night goggles, along with his gun. As he pulled his jacket back over his arm, he saw the bloodstain.

Shit.

Angry at himself for missing it, his thoughts returned to the man in the car and how he'd flashed his phone at him.

Had he seen the blood?

Mitch decided if he had, he'd be hearing sirens all around him by now.

Grabbing a different jacket, he snuck outside to the tree stand he'd installed early in the summer, and climbed up. Although Mitch wasn't a hunter, he'd thought the hunting stand was a neat idea, considering the fact that there was a lot of wildlife around and it gave him a great view of the river. He'd never dreamed he'd be using it to catch a trespasser.

Settling into the mesh chair, he stared toward the entrance of his property and waited. As he scoured the darkness for the intruder's return, his paranoia resurfaced.

What if he was all wrong about the guy? What if he was actually with the Russians?

Mitch wasn't an idiot and knew they'd be looking for him eventually, too. Fortunately, Kurt had hidden Mitch's true identity from Yury. At least, that's what he'd told him. For all he knew, that was a crock of shit and they were already on his tail. But if the intruder had been part of their circle, Mitch knew he'd be dead by now.

The sound of twigs snapping startled him. Heart racing, he turned toward the noise and saw him.

The man *had* ignored his warning.

He'd returned.

Shaking with anger, Mitch watched as the stranger snuck through the trees and slowly made his way over to the house. When he went around to the other side of the building, Mitch climbed down the tree, prepared to add another tick to his body count. Although he'd been pretty certain of his return, it still made his blood boil that someone was on his property and spying.

He took the gun out of his pocket and crept around the building after him. When Mitch rounded the corner, he saw the man climbing the deck and thought he might be breaking in. But a few seconds later, the stranger came back down.

Raising the gun, Mitch surprised him at the bottom.

"Whoa," the stranger said, raising his hands in the air.

"I told you to get off my property," Mitch snapped. "Do you realize I could shoot you right now and never step foot behind bars?"

"Maybe. Maybe not," he replied. "I'm not here to threaten you."

"Then who in the hell are you and what do you want?"

"I told you before, I lost my dog."

Mitch grunted. "And you think he's up on my deck or in the house?"

He smiled weakly. "Hell, I don't know. He's a cute dog. Maybe you decided to keep him."

"I've had enough of this bullshit. Let me see some I.D.," he replied.

The man began reaching for his wallet when Mitch realized he could also have a gun.

"Wait a second. Hands in the air," he snapped. "I'll grab it."

Sighing, the other man raised his hands.

"Try anything funny and you'll never see your *dog* again," he said dryly before holding his pistol up to the man's face. Reaching around, he pulled his wallet out of his back pocket and stepped back.

"Nice place you've got here, by the way," said the man, looking past him at the house. "I imagine living right next to the river costs a pretty penny?"

Ignoring him, Mitch opened up the man's wallet. "Dustin Frazer," he said, reading the driver's license. "Looks like your

224

home address is a long ways from Stillwater. Why would your dog be out in these parts?"

"We were doing some traveling. I had to let him out to pee on the way home."

Mitch grunted. "You have an answer for everything, don't you?"

"Not everything. I'm trying to figure out why you're still holding a gun to my face."

"Trespassing," he replied, holding the wallet out to him.

Dustin reached for it, but Mitch let go before he was able to grab it. The wallet dropped into the snow, some of its contents spilling out.

"What's that?" Mitch asked coldly as Dustin bent down to retrieve his stuff.

"What does it look like?" mumbled Dustin, hastily grabbing the picture of Lainey that had also slipped out.

"It looks like you have a picture of someone I know who's missing," Mitch replied, glaring at him.

"Really? I have no idea of what you're talking about."

Furious, Mitch shoved him backward. "Don't bullshit me. I *know* that's Beth's kid, Lainey. Why in the hell are you here?"

Dustin looked him in the eye. "To see if you know anything about the case."

"Why would I?" he replied angrily. "I hardly ever see her."

Suddenly, Dustin's eyes widened as he stared past him, at the house.

Mitch turned around and saw Sammy peeking down at them from an upstairs window.

The boy quickly disappeared.

Shit.

Dustin's face turned to stone. "Who's that?"

225

"You ask too many questions."

"Was it Lainey?" He took a step toward the window. "Do you have her in the house?"

In answer, Mitch shot him in the chest.

Chapter 47

Carissa

CARISSA SEARCHED ALL over until she found Anna Dubov's card. She called and was about to leave a message, when the woman answered.

"Hi. I'm sorry I'm calling so late and… you might not remember me, but my name is Carissa Jones and we spoke awhile back."

"I remember you," Dubov said, sounding tired. "You helped in the Stephen Cutler case. You're the psychic."

"Yes," Carissa replied, relieved that she'd remembered. "Anyway, I don't know if you heard, but I've been trying to help locate Lainey Brown—"

"Yes. I heard. Have you come up with something?" she asked, sounding more awake.

Carissa told her what she suspected and was pleasantly surprised to find that Dubov didn't immediately brush her off.

"Well, the videotape showed that Lainey knew her kidnapper," Dubov said. "And so I definitely think it's something to look into."

"He was also in town during Lainey's kidnapping and that little boy's disappearance. Sammy."

"I doubt they're related, but you never know," said Dubov. She let out a sigh. "So, you think he might have Lainey with him now?"

227

"Honestly, yes. I really do."

"I find it hard to believe that he would have her at his house, even if he is involved. The surveillance tapes showed that her kidnapper put her into an SUV, so there are others involved as well. She could be halfway across the world right now," Dubov said. "Especially if she's being trafficked, which we believe."

"I think he's involved with the trafficking. I also believe something might have gone wrong," Carissa replied.

Dubov was silent for several seconds and then told her she'd do what she could.

"Are you going over there tonight?" Carissa asked, hopeful.

"Unfortunately, I'm not going to be able to get a search warrant, especially at this time. It's very late."

Her heart sank. "Yes, but time is obviously of the essence," she said, the line sounding funny coming from her lips. But it was the truth. The clock was ticking.

"I know. I know. Look, Ms. Jones, I'll see what I can do. I can't promise you anything tonight, but in the morning, I'll drive over myself and talk to the man. My gut is telling me you're really onto something."

Carissa knew it was all she could hope for. Especially since there wasn't any evidence pointing directly toward Mitch. And the fact that the woman wasn't ruling out her accusations was a relief.

"Thank you," Carissa said.

"Of course. Now, if something else comes up, feel free to call me."

"Definitely. Thank you for not brushing this off."

"No problem. I want to find Lainey, and believe you have a gift, Ms. Jones. I'm sure you get a lot of doubters, but I'm not one of them."

"Thank you. I appreciate that."

"Of course."

They spoke for a few seconds more and then hung up.

Carissa went back to bed, and even though the conversation she'd had with Dubov was promising, the feeling of impending doom became worse as the minutes on the clock ticked by. By two a.m. she was too distraught to sleep and knew, with absolute certainty, that something was about to go terribly wrong and it involved Dustin.

Picking up her phone, she sent him a text.

Is everything okay?

She waited. When he didn't respond, she sent another one. And then a third.

Still, there was no reply.

Maybe he'd left his phone in the car?

She hoped it was the case, but couldn't see Dustin doing that. He'd forget his wallet over his cell phone.

Worried sick, she thought about calling Dubov back, but decided against it. For all Carissa knew, she was overreacting and of course, Dustin didn't need to be cited for trespassing.

Deciding to take matters into her own hands, Carissa quickly dressed and grabbed her keys. As angry as Dustin might get with her showing up, she just couldn't ignore the gnawing in her gut.

A short time later as she was getting into her SUV, Carissa thought about her Ruger. Although she'd never used it in defense, something told her it would be idiotic not to bring protection. Especially if Mitch really was the criminal she thought him to be.

She ran back into the house and grabbed the gun from the safe. Trembling at the thought of having to actually use it, she shoved it into her purse and hurried back to her truck.

TWENTY-FIVE MINUTES later, and with still no word from Dustin, Carissa drove slowly down the side-streets near Mitch's home. As she came up to the path leading to his private driveway, she decided not to take it, and drove up another couple of blocks. There, she parked her SUV and tried texting him once again. After waiting around for several minutes, she got out of her vehicle and began walking toward Mitch's property.

Chapter 48

Lainey

"IT'S YOUR FAULT I shot that man," Mitch snapped at Sammy. "He's dead because of *you*."

Lainey and Sammy were huddled in the corner of the wine cellar together, crying. They'd heard the commotion outside, which was why Sammy had snuck upstairs and peeked out one of the windows.

"I'm sorry!" sobbed Sammy, his face wet with tears.

Lainey thought Mitch, who was pacing back and forth in the wine cellar, looked almost like a wild man. He was certainly acting different than earlier. Now his hair was sticking straight up from pulling at it, and his eyes were bloodshot.

"You're *sorry*," Mitch sneered and then giggled. "Honestly, he deserved it, though."

Lainey glanced over at Sammy, who was just as dumbfounded as she was. One moment Mitch was angry. The next, he appeared almost happy. It made no sense.

Talking to himself, Mitch continued pacing the room in his wet boots. "I need to get rid of his body. I don't know where his truck is, though. Where in the hell did he leave it?" Stopping abruptly, he ran a hand over his face and looked at the kids. "Stay here, and if

231

you so much as move from that spot, I will shoot you both in your knees. You'll never walk, let alone run, again. You got that?"

Sammy and Lainey both nodded quickly.

"I'll be back soon," he said, leaving them alone again.

They listened as he hurried up the staircase and went outside.

"What do you think he's doing?" whispered Lainey after a few minutes.

Sammy ran the back of his hand across his face, to dry his tears. "I don't know," he mumbled, wrapping his arms around his knees. "I wish he would leave and never come back."

"Me, too."

"And I wish I would have never looked out the window," he whispered.

"You didn't know."

Sammy's lip trembled. "I should have known, though. He's nuts."

Nodding, Lainey sighed. "Do you think he's going to bring us home still?"

Sammy snorted. "Heck no. I think he's lying."

Lainey nodded. "I think so, too."

Exhausted and frightened, the two waited for Mitch to return, and it took some time. When he finally walked back into the wine cellar, they'd both dozed off again on the air mattress.

Mitch clapped his hands. "Up… up! Let's go!"

"Where are we going?" Lainey squeaked, sitting up.

His eyes bored into Sammy's. "Since this one here screwed everything for us, we need to get rid of the body. So, let's go," he said, waving his hand impatiently.

Lainey and Sammy stood up.

Mitch looked down at their feet. "That's right. Well, I've got some slippers upstairs."

They followed him out of the cellar and up the stairs. He opened up a closet and pulled out a pair of brown suede slippers. He handed them to Sammy. "Put those on. As for you," he looked at Lainey. "I guess I don't have anything. Just, try not to step in any puddles in the garage."

Sammy slid the slippers on. They were much too big, but Mitch told him to keep them on.

"It's better than nothing. Now, let's go," he said.

Mitch guided them through the kitchen and into the garage, where an older, black truck was parked. Both kids stopped and gaped at the vehicle.

"Where did that come from?" Sammy asked.

"It's the dead guy's. He thought he was tricky and parked it up the street. But I found it," Mitch said, looking proud of himself. He opened up the passenger door. "Get in."

There was a long bench seat in the front and the two climbed onto it.

Mitch shut the door and went around. He got in and started the engine. As he was pulling out of the garage, he stomped on the brake and swore. "I forgot something." He looked at Sammy. "I don't trust you. You're coming back inside with me. And you," he glanced down at Lainey, who was seated in the middle. "If you try leaving by yourself, I'll kill your friend here. Understand?"

Swallowing, Lainey nodded.

"Let's go," ordered Mitch, opening his door.

Sammy got out and followed him back into the house while Lainey watched. As she waited for them to return, she saw movement out of the corner of her eye. Turning her head, Lainey gasped when a red-haired woman appeared at the side of the truck.

233

Chapter 49

Carissa

STUNNED AT WHO was sitting inside Dustin's vehicle, Carissa opened up the door. "Lainey?"

The little girl nodded.

She heaved a sigh of relief. "Oh, thank God. Where is Dustin, I mean, the man who owns this truck?"

"I don't know," Lainey said.

Carissa's heart stopped. She'd seen Mitch leave the truck and go inside.

Where in the hell was Dustin?

"Did you see him?"

"Mitch?"

It was clear the little girl had no idea what Carissa was talking about. Knowing time was running out, she held out her hand. "Come on, let's go."

Lainey's eyes widened. "I can't go. Mitch said he'll kill Sammy if I leave."

"He's not going to kill him," Carissa said, noticing Lainey was dressed oddly and not wearing shoes.

"Yes, he is. He said so."

"He just told you that so you'd behave. Come on," she said, reaching inside and pulling her into her arms. As she was about to

234

Looking for Lainey   Kristen Middleton

carry Lainey away from the truck, Carissa heard sounds coming from underneath the truck's bed-cover.

"Carissa!?"

"Oh my God, Dustin?" she gasped, rushing to the back of the truck. Setting Lainey down, she opened up the tailgate and found him lying inside. From the pained look on his face, she could tell he was hurt. "Are you okay?"

Before he could answer, Mitch's voice rang out inside the garage. Fortunately, he was talking to Sammy and hadn't yet noticed what was happening.

"Get her out of here," Dustin whispered, nodding toward Lainey.

Frightened, Carissa picked up the little girl and began running away from the truck.

"Hey!" hollered Mitch.

She looked back over her shoulder and saw him rushing toward her. Knowing she couldn't outrun Mitch, Carissa got behind a tree, set Lainey down, and reached for her Ruger.

Mitch rounded the corner and his eyes widened in surprise. "Drop it!" he snapped, aiming his revolver at her.

"The… The police are on their way, Mitch," she said in a shaky voice. "They know you kidnapped Lainey."

"Bullshit," he sneered. "Let me guess, you're the nosy psychic?"

"Put your gun down," she said, trying not to let him see how shaky her hand was.

"You don't have the guts to shoot," he said, smiling.

"To save her, I do," Carissa said.

Mitch studied her face for a few seconds and then looked at Lainey. "Come to me. *Now*. If you want to see Sammy alive again."

The sudden snap of a twig behind Mitch caused everyone to look.

235

"Drop your weapon!" Detective Dubov ordered, staring hard at Mitch.

"Who the hell are you?" he growled, aiming his gun at her now.

"Police. Throw down your weapon." Dubov said. "Don't be a fool."

Carissa knew he was going to pull the trigger. She grabbed Lainey and shoved her down toward the ground as gunfire erupted around them.

Chapter 50

Dustin

DUSTIN CRAWLED OUT of the back of the truck. Wincing in pain, he dropped to his feet and was about to go after Mitch, when he saw a boy crouched behind the air conditioning unit.

"Hey," he said, moving toward him slowly. "Are you Sammy?"

"Yes," replied the kid in a frightened voice.

"Don't be afraid. I'm here to help you."

Sammy stood up.

Dustin thought about the boathouse, which had been open earlier. "You need to find a better hiding spot. Tell you what, there's a boathouse in back. Run back there and wait for me. When it's safe, I'll come and get you."

Sammy looked unsure.

"Hurry up. Before Mitch comes back."

Eyes widening, Sammy disappeared behind the house.

Letting out a ragged breath, Dustin headed toward the trees, relieved he'd worn a bulletproof vest under his clothing. He was bruised badly and his ribcage felt like it was on fire, but he was alive. He could only hope Carissa and Lainey were okay.

When Dustin reached the woods, he heard the sounds of guns going off and Lainey crying out.

Crouching down, Dustin snuck through the trees and let out a sigh of relief when he found Mitch lying in the snow, bloody and unmoving. Standing above him was Detective Anna Dubov, her gun still smoking. A few yards away from them was Carissa and Lainey.

It was over.

Seeing Dustin approach, tears filled Carissa's eyes. She rushed to his side and threw her arms around his neck. "Dustin."

"Careful," he replied, wincing.

"Are you okay?"

"I've been shot," Dustin said through clenched teeth.

Carissa released him. "You're shot? Where?"

Dustin showed her the hole in his jacket. "He got me right here." He grinned. "Luckily, I took your warning seriously and put on my Kevlar vest."

She smiled in relief. "Thank goodness."

"Let's just hope this was the premonition you've been worried about," he replied.

"I don't know if it is, so don't you dare take any unnecessary chances in the future," Carissa said sternly.

"I won't. So, is he really dead?" Dustin asked the detective. There was a lot of blood coming from the bullet wound in his stomach, but that didn't always mean anything.

"It looks that way. I got him a couple of times," Dubov replied, kicking away Mitch's gun. She bent down and felt for a pulse. "Yep. Looks like he's gone."

Dustin looked over at Lainey. It was obvious from the look on her face that the child was in shock. "We'd better get her out of here," he said, moving toward the child.

"Where's Sammy?" Carissa asked, looking past him toward the house.

238

"I told him to hide until it was safe," he replied and looked down at Lainey. "I bet you want to go and see your mommy and daddy," he said softly.

Lainey looked up at him and nodded.

"I know they're going to be thrilled when they find out you're okay." He looked down at her feet and his eyes widened. "Jesus, we need to get her some shoes. Your feet must be freezing."

She looked down at her socks. "I can barely feel them."

"I'll take care of it," Detective Dubov said. She walked over to Lainey and smiled warmly. "I have some warm blankets in my car. Let's get you out of the cold and home to your parents, okay?"

Lainey's eyes lit up. "Okay."

Smiling, Dubov picked her up. "Could you find Sammy, too? I want to get them home to their parents as soon as I can. They must be traumatized after everything that's happened."

"Of course," said Dustin.

Dubov reached for her phone. "I'll call this in and let Samuels know."

"Thanks for doing that."

She nodded. "Hey, it's my job. Besides, I'm sure they're going to want statements from all of us," replied Dubov.

Chapter 51

Carissa

ONCE BOTH CHILDREN were settled into Anna Dubov's vehicle, the detective thanked Carissa for her help in finding the children.

"No problem. I was shocked to see you here," Carissa replied. "And relieved, of course."

"I couldn't stop thinking about everything, so I *had* to come out here and inspect things for myself. Psychics aren't the only ones who sometimes rely on their gut instincts," Dubov said with a smile.

"Good thing you did. He was about to shoot me," Carissa said.

"It looked that way, although you were holding your own pretty well," she replied.

"Are you kidding? My hand was shaking so bad, I'm surprised I didn't shoot myself," Carissa said.

"I assume you have a permit for that gun you were holding?" Dubov said.

"Of course," she replied, her cheeks heating up.

Dubov laughed. "Relax. I'm just teasing you."

Carissa smiled.

"Anyway, I'm surprised you didn't call Samuels." Dubov looked at Dustin. "He mentioned that you two worked in the same precinct, a few years ago."

He nodded. "I actually called him before I got out here," said Dustin with a wry smile. "He was going to drop by and interview Mitch in the morning."

"That would have been too late," Dubov said.

"Yeah, I told him that. Make sure *you* give him shit about it, too," Dustin said. "I know I will."

"Definitely. I left him a message so he's been made aware of the situation," Dubov replied. "And the cops should be here any minute. How are you doing, by the way?"

Dustin shrugged. "I'll be fine. Bruised."

Dubov grinned. "I'm sure. That had to hurt like hell."

He touched his chest and winced. "It feels like someone hit me in the chest with a hammer."

"How *did* you manage to get yourself shot?" Carissa asked him.

"After I got off the phone with you, Mitch showed up and confronted me. He told me to get off his property. Which I did. But, of course I came back," Dustin replied and smiled. "I guess I learned my lesson for trespassing when he shot me."

"Well, thank goodness you're good at playing dead," said Dubov with an amused look on her face.

"I acted a little in high school," he replied and chuckled. "In fact, I once played a zombie."

Dubov nodded. "Impressive."

"Not really. All I had to do was moan and stumble around," he replied. "Like I was drunk. I might be doing that later to numb the pain."

She laughed and then looked at her cell phone. "It's really late. I should probably get these kids home."

"Did you call their parents?" Carissa asked.

241

Dubov nodded. "Yeah. I did. They're ecstatic and can't wait to see them. Anyway, thanks again for helping with the case."

"It was our pleasure," Dustin said.

They said their goodbyes and the detective got into her car. As she was pulling away, Dustin crossed his arms over his chest and frowned.

"What is it?" Carissa asked, raising an eyebrow.

"I was just thinking that the department must be paying her a ton of dough. That was a Mercedes S450. Fully loaded, too, from what I could tell."

"Oh?" Carissa didn't know much about cars, let alone a Mercedes. She did know that they were out of her price-range, however.

"Yeah. It's a new one, too. They're over one-hundred grand."

Carissa's eyes widened. "Wow."

"Exactly. *Wow*."

"Maybe she's married to someone who helped buy her the car?" said Carissa. "Someone rich."

He smirked. "You tell me. You're the psychic."

She'd been so relieved to find the children that Carissa hadn't thought much about Dubov or her fancy car. It also seemed a little odd that the detective was taking the children home so quickly.

Dustin patted his jacket and swore. "Dammit. That's right. Mitch took my phone. I was thinking maybe I should call Samuels myself."

"I'm sure he's on his way," Carissa said, hoping that lack of sleep was just making them both paranoid.

"Maybe, but I wonder what's taking him, and the police, so long to get here?" he said, turning toward the road.

She wondered the same thing.

"Oh. Here comes someone," Dustin said.

They watched as a black SUV slowly turned down the driveway and headed toward them. Alarm bells went off in Carissa's head.

She grabbed Dustin's arm. "That's not the police. We've got to get out of here."

Looking just as concerned, Dustin backed up and then the two of them began to run in the opposite direction.

Chapter 52

Dubov

AS ANNA DUBOV turned off Mitch's long driveway, she flashed her lights at the Tahoe waiting patiently up the street. It approached and then turned down the path she just left to clean up the mess Hawk had made.

Relaxing for the first time all night, Anna looked in her rearview mirror and saw that both children had fallen asleep. This was also a relief, considering that she wasn't driving them home. She was taking them far away, to a new location. One where they couldn't escape. Of course, now that her cousin Yury was dead, Anna imagined that the organization would be much more careful whom they left the children with. She never liked or trusted Kurt, and as for her cousin, he'd always been sloppy. Truthfully, although they were related, she was glad he was gone. He'd always been a stubborn and arrogant hothead. Finding both him and Dina dead in his rental car had taken a load off her shoulders.

Anna's phone rang. It was Samuels. Swearing under her breath, she answered it.

"Sorry to call you so late, but I just received word that Mitch Olson's truck was found abandoned in a rural area in Scandia," he said.

244

"Who's that?" she asked quietly, glancing again at the sleeping children.

"Beth Brown's fiancé's brother," he said.

"Oh. So, you think this has something to do with the case?"

"Actually, I'm starting to." He told her about the phone call he'd received earlier from Dustin.

"Interesting," she replied, yawning. "Although, abandoning a vehicle is a far stretch from being involved in a kidnapping."

"Not when two dead bodies were also found at a farmhouse up the road from where his truck was found."

Anna tried to remain calm. They wanted Mitch to take the fall for the kidnapping and murders, but nobody had suspected that Samuels or the police would catch on so soon. And as far as the bodies went, they'd disposed of Yury's and Dina's, so she wasn't sure exactly who he was talking about. Then there was Kurt, who was missing. She thought he may have bolted, considering she'd learned that he'd been longtime friends with Mitch. He was still a problem, however. One they needed to find and fix.

"What bodies are you talking about?" she asked.

"Edgar and Wilma Dunn. An older couple found brutally murdered. And that's not all…"

Great. What else? "What do you mean?"

"Their vehicle was recovered in a ditch, up the road. In the trunk they found the body of a man named Kurt Hastings and a teenager, who they're still trying to I.D."

She was relieved that Kurt was dead. Considering Tara was missing, she figured that's who he'd been found with.

"Really?"

"Fortunately, the girl is alive, but unconscious. Anyway, I just learned that some units have been dispatched and are on their way to Mitch Olson's."

Shit. "Okay."

245

"I'm headed toward Scandia right now. Apparently Kurt Hastings was renting a farmhouse up the road from the Dunn's."

"Alright."

"I know it's late, but do you want to meet me out there?"

"In Scandia?"

"Yeah."

"I suppose. It might take me awhile."

"No problem. I'm sure Forensics will be there for hours."

In the distance, she could already hear the sound of sirens.

Shit. Shit. Shit.

"I have to go. I'll see you soon," she told Samuels.

"Okay."

Hanging up, she pulled her car over and sent a message to the driver of the Tahoe.

The police are OTW. Abort.

Chapter 53

Carissa

THEY RAN THROUGH the woods, the plan being to get to Carissa's SUV. Unfortunately, Dustin's injuries slowed them down.

"Dammit," he growled, slipping on a patch of ice. He fell down hard, gasping in pain as he hit the ground.

Carissa helped him up.

Behind them, they could hear the echo of doors opening and closing.

"I can't outrun them," Dustin said. "Do you still have your gun?"

"Yes."

He held out his hand. "Give it to me. I'll cover you."

She gave him a dirty look. "No!" she whispered angrily. "I'm not leaving you behind."

"If both of us die, there won't be any justice. Nobody will know what happened to Lainey and Sammy. Now, give me your weapon," he said sharply.

Sighing, she handed him the Ruger. "I'm still not leaving you, Dustin. So, you can give up the heroic talk."

Mumbling to himself, he pulled her behind a tree and they watched as three burly men headed in their direction with flashlights. When they were almost upon them, Dustin raised the Ruger.

"Hold up," one of the men said. He pulled out his phone and swore.

"What is it?" asked one of them in a thick Russian accent.

"We're to abort," he replied, shoving his phone back into his pocket. "Quickly."

"What? Why?" snapped the third man.

Sirens rang out in the distance, answering the question for him.

The three men ran back to the Tahoe, and seconds later, the vehicle was flying back down the driveway.

"LET ME GET this straight… Detective *Dubov* has the children?" Samuels said, staring at them in disbelief.

"Yes. She said she was taking them home," Dustin replied. "Obviously, she isn't."

Frowning, he took out his cell phone, punched in some numbers, and cleared his throat. "Anna, call me as soon as you get this message."

Carissa felt sick to her stomach. The children were once again lost to them. She just knew it.

"Dubov set this up," she said, touching Dustin's arm. "I'd stake my life on it that she's involved with the trafficking. That's why the men in the Tahoe had arrived so quickly. They were waiting for her to take the kids away so they could get rid of us."

Samuels snorted. "Dubov? A child abductor? Come on. There's got to be a logical explanation to this that doesn't involve my partner being a criminal," he said gruffly.

"It's the truth," Carissa said angrily. The man wouldn't take her seriously if his life depended on it. "Why else would she have Lainey and Sammy without telling you?"

248

"You did say you spoke to her a short time ago. Don't you think it's odd that she didn't mention being here?" added Dustin. "Or, that she killed Mitch? I mean, even you can't come up with a good enough reason for her to leave the scene of a crime, especially when she was involved in the shooting."

From the look on his face, Carissa knew he was wondering the same thing.

"It's not protocol, I'll give you that. She's definitely acting strangely." Pulling out his phone once again, he placed another call.

Carissa sighed in relief. At least the man wasn't too stubborn to realize that something was definitely not adding up.

"It's Samuels. Put out an APB for Detective Anna Dubov. She was last seen driving her white Mercedes. No, I don't have the license plate number. You'll have to look it up," he said into the phone.

"I wonder if we should call Lainey's parents," said Dustin.

"No," Samuels said, hanging up his cell. "Let us handle this. We don't know for sure that Mike isn't in on this as well. And we don't want to panic them. Especially since we don't know what the hell is going on."

"I don't think Mike is involved," Carissa said.

Samuels looked like he was about to reply, but must have thought better of it. Instead, he asked if they could meet him down at the station.

"After you get your chest looked at," he added. "You must be in godawful pain right now."

Dustin shrugged. "I'm alive. Thanks to her." He put his arm around Carissa's shoulders, wincing as he moved. "She saw it coming."

Carissa looked up at him. "Hopefully, this is the one I saw. Just keep your vest handy for future cases."

"Yes, ma'am," he replied before kissing her on the lips.

249

Samuels' cell phone went off. He answered it and they watched as a look of relief swept over his face. They spoke for a few more seconds and then he hung up.

"Tara, the girl they brought into the hospital earlier, is conscious and talking. I'm going to head there right now and see if she can give us any information on this case. Apparently, as soon as she woke up, she began asking about Lainey and Sammy."

"She was abducted by them, too," Carissa said, staring off into space.

"That's what she told one of our officers," Samuels said, nodding.

"We want to come with you," Dustin said firmly. "To the hospital."

"I don't think that's a good idea," Samuels said, frowning.

"Bullshit. You need us right now. Especially Carissa. If anyone is going to find those kids, it's going to be her," Dustin replied. "She's the one who knew about Mitch before anyone."

Sighing, Samuels nodded reluctantly. "Fine. Let's go."

Chapter 54

Dubov

DUBOV KNEW SHE was in hot water. Samuels was already calling her, and soon, if not already, he'd realize that she was involved.

Everything was falling apart.

Although she'd planned for a potential fallout like this, Anna hadn't actually thought she'd get caught. It wasn't as if she'd ever had to get directly involved in any of the kidnappings. Her job was to steer the investigations away from the organization, should anyone ever get close. And tonight, she'd made an error in judgement. One that now put her on the run. Even worse, she had to leave her plush lifestyle and relocate somewhere, possibly even out of the country, which wasn't just inconvenient. It was a total nightmare.

Trying to remain calm, she continued on her way toward the small, private airport in Mankato, where the three of them would be whisked away. To where, she didn't even know yet.

Sighing, she glanced back at the sleeping children. For them, she felt nothing, which she knew most would find cold and heartless. Especially knowing what their future held. But Anna had long ago stopped caring for anyone but herself, back in Grozny.

As a child, she'd lived there with her mother, Helga, and stepfather, Vitaly, who'd been a cold-hearted monster. For years, they were his punching bags and it wasn't until Viktor, his brother—and a member of the Russian mafia—decided Vitaly was too volatile for the organization and assassinated him. Anna and Helga were then recruited into the family business, and were promised protection and more wealth than they could ever dream of. After being beaten down for so many years, it sounded like paradise, and that's when Anna pretty much sold herself to the devil. Two years later, when she turned sixteen, he moved Anna to Minnesota to live with relatives and become 'Americanized'. Once she graduated from high school, they pressured her into law enforcement, which Viktor claimed would be the best use for her. So she joined the police academy, and from there, took the necessary steps, which led her to where she was now.

Which is now nothing, she thought miserably.

Her career was over and Anna knew Viktor would be furious when he found out how sloppy everyone had been. She wasn't looking forward to facing him. Her role in the business had been invaluable, and now, they were all at risk. Anyone with connections to her would be investigated.

At least she still had the two children.

There was no way she was leaving Minnesota without them. They'd been the cause of all the trouble, and to show up empty-handed, without the little brats, would cause her even more trouble.

Chapter 55

Carissa

TARA WAS ASLEEP when they arrived at the hospital. Next to her sat a woman with a tear-stained face who introduced herself as the teenager's mother, Carol. She stood up and made them follow her into the hallway.

"She's already answered enough questions," argued the woman when they asked to interview her. "Let her sleep."

"We don't have time," Samuels said firmly. "Two children are missing and Tara might be able to help us locate them."

"The police asked her if she knew where the kids were and she had no idea," she replied angrily. "For the love of God, please leave her alone. She's already been through so much."

Carissa sensed that Carol hadn't seen her daughter for a very long time and was frightened more than anything that she'd be taken away from her again.

"Just a couple of questions," Carissa said softly. "I know Tara would do anything to save those kids and might be angry if she's not given the chance."

Studying her face, Carol frowned. "Who are you?"

Carissa told her.

"I thought you looked familiar," she replied in a tired voice. "I saw you on the news. You found that girl up near Duluth."

253

Carissa smiled sadly. "Yes."

The woman let out a ragged sigh. "Fine. But just a couple of questions, and if she gets upset, you'll need to leave."

"Of course," Carissa replied.

Carol allowed them back into the room and gently woke up Tara.

"Honey, the police are here again. They have more questions for you. If you don't think you're up to it, I'll send them away," Carol said softly.

Tara's eyes fluttered open. She looked at the three of them and licked her lips. "What do you want to know?"

Samuels began asking her about the farmhouse and the people who had kidnapped her.

"I told the other officer all about that," said Tara, looking exhausted.

The detective was about to say something when Carissa cleared her throat. "Can I ask her a few things?"

Samuels nodded.

Carissa stepped closer to Tara and gently laid her hand on the girl's. "You were very brave, helping them earlier," she said.

"Maybe. But, they're still missing so it was probably a waste of time," Tara mumbled.

"No. It's not," Carissa said. "Because of you, we have gotten closer to finding them than ever before. You have to believe that."

Tara's eyes filled with tears. "Do you think they're okay?"

Carissa nodded. "I do. They're with a woman now. Her name is Anna. Does that ring a bell with you?"

Tara bit her lower lip. "I remember Yury talking to someone on the phone before with that name. You think she has the children?"

"Yes." Carissa closed her eyes and concentrated on Tara. Searching for something that might lead to finding Lainey and

254

Sammy. Suddenly, she opened her eyes. "Did Yury ever mention anything about an escape route? Or a way to get out of Minnesota in a hurry if they needed to?"

Tara was quiet for a few minutes and then her eyes widened. "No, but I know they used some airfield in Mankato sometimes. To fly the children out of the state."

Samuels pulled out his phone. "Anna has talked about Mankato before. I think she might have lived there as a teenager," he said excitedly.

Carissa's gut told her they were headed in the right direction. "Everything has fallen apart for her. She can't stay in her car for very long and needs to get out of the state. Maybe even the country. It's literally her only way out of this. You need to check out all of the private airports in Mankato."

"I doubt there are too many of those in that area." Samuels looked at her and grunted. "Lady, for the first time ever, I think you and I are exactly on the same page."

Chapter 56

Dubov

IT TOOK ANNA two hours to reach Bower's Airport, which was owned by the family who'd taken her in when Viktor had shipped her to America. By the time she arrived, the sun was peeking over the horizon. Unfortunately, the lights were all out at the airfield and the gate was locked.

Frustrated, Anna picked up her cell phone and began dialing the owner's number. She'd spoken to him earlier, explaining the situation, and he'd promised to fly her out of Minnesota himself.

"Abe, we're here, and you're not. Call me. Better yet, get your ass to the airfield," she said angrily before hanging up.

"What are we doing here?" asked Sammy, just waking up.

Anna looked at him over her shoulder. "We're going for a ride. Have you ever been on a plane before?"

"No," he said, looking outside. "I thought we were going home?"

"You are going home. But first we want to get you on an airplane so that you're safe."

He frowned.

She forced a smile to her face as the lies slid off her tongue. If there was one thing Anna was good at, it was making things up. "You see, the kidnappers are trying to find you and that's why we're flying you far away. Where they can't. Once we know you're safe, you'll see your mommies and daddies."

"I always wanted to go on a plane," Lainey said, her eyes fluttering open. "Where is it?"

"Good question," she muttered dryly, looking out the windshield again. Anna pointed toward the three large buildings on the other side of the fence. "I'm sure our plane is in one of those hangars."

"Cool," said Sammy.

Frustrated and anxious, Anna pulled out a pack of cigarettes from her purse. "I'm going outside to have a smoke. You guys wait in here."

"Okay," said Lainey.

"I have to go to the bathroom," Sammy said.

Anna sighed. *Kids.* "What about you, Lainey?"

"I'm okay," she replied. "But, I'm thirsty."

"We'll take care of that on the plane. Sammy, you're going to have to pee in the bushes over there," Anna said, pointing by the fence. "Think you can you handle that?"

"I guess," he replied glumly.

"Let's go," she said.

Anna and Sammy got out of the car. She lit a cigarette and watched as the boy made his way over to the bushes. When he found a spot, he looked back at Anna.

"It's okay. Just do it," she said.

His cheeks turned pink. "I don't think I can."

She sighed. "Sorry. I won't look."

Sammy looked relieved. "Thanks."

Anna turned around and was about to take another puff of her cigarette when she heard a helicopter in the distance. Frowning, she looked around until she spotted it.

And... it was coming in fast.

She gasped, noticing it was a State Patrol helicopter and headed directly toward them. "Sammy, let's go!"

"I'm not finished yet," he said, his back to her. Hearing the helicopter, he also looked up into the sky. "Wow, cool!"

"Shit. Shit. Shit!" Anna said, throwing down her cigarette. "Sammy! Come on!"

"Are those the good guys or the bad guys?" he asked, scratching his cheek.

The helicopter moved right above them, hovering.

Unwilling to wait for Sammy any longer, Anna jumped in the car and backed away from the gate.

"Wait, what about Sammy?" cried Lainey as they sped off.

"Quiet," snapped Anna.

Squad cars appeared in the distance in front of her as she raced away from the airport. Slamming on the brakes, she turned the car around and headed in the opposite direction.

"I'm scared. Why are we running from the police?" Lainey cried.

"Just, shut up!" Anna hollered, staring above at the helicopter as it circled around and began following her.

Lainey sunk farther down into the seat, terrified.

"I'm so stupid… stupid… stupid…" Anna shrieked. "I should have known better!"

She knew she couldn't outrun them. She also knew she'd go to jail, where Viktor would pay someone to silence her forever. Their operation was too big and a small fry like her wasn't worth the risk.

I'm dead.

No matter what happens, I'm dead.

Anna's eyes filled with tears as two more squads appeared in front of her. They were going to block her in.

"It's not worth it," she said, imagining how it would be for her in prison. Always waiting for someone to strike.

258

Would they kill her in the showers?
Would someone stab her in the middle of the night?

Knowing Viktor, he would make sure it happened right away. It would be painful. Agonizing. A slow death to remind her of how she'd failed him.

"I'm scared!" Lainey cried as Anna stomped on the gas.

If I'm going to die, I want it to be quick…

"Mommy!" the little girl whimpered in the backseat.

"I'm sorry. It's better this way," she said in a hollow voice as their vehicle barreled toward the patrol cars. "And nobody can hurt you… or me… ever… again."

Lainey screamed.

Chapter 57

Carissa

CARISSA STARED DOWN in horror as Anna's vehicle collided with the squad car. Over the noise of the chopper, they could still hear the violence of the wreckage as both front ends were crushed in a collision that had to have been fatal to everyone involved.

"Lainey must have been in there," Dustin said in a thick voice. "Good Lord, what was that woman thinking?"

The pilot landed the helicopter and the three of them raced out and headed to the wreckage, where police were already trying to get everyone out.

"Is Lainey okay?" Carissa cried, not seeing any movement from the backseat of the Mercedes.

"It's hard to tell," said one of the officers. "There's gas leaking everywhere and we need to get them out as soon as possible. Please, stay back."

She watched as they worked on opening up the back doors of the Mercedes to try and get to Lainey.

"The driver has no pulse," one of the other officers said as he felt Anna's neck.

One didn't have to be psychic to see that the detective was dead. The entire front end of her car was crushed and there was too much blood on her and the airbag.

"That's what she wanted," mumbled Carissa. Although she had no love for the dead woman, she felt Anna had chosen death over something much more frightening, and in a way, she pitied her.

"Thank goodness. They got the back door open," Dustin said, stepping forward to try and get a better look.

Carissa watched breathlessly as they carefully pulled Lainey out of the back. They set her down on a blanket gently and began checking her pulse.

"Is she okay?" Detective Samuels asked, also shaken.

"She has a weak pulse and… it looks like she hit her head pretty hard," said the officer. "Other than that, we'll have to wait for the paramedics to learn more."

Carissa's eyes filled with tears as they worked on the little girl. Soon, the paramedics arrived and they took over.

"What's wrong with her? Is she going to be okay?" asked Sammy, pulling away from an officer who'd been trying to comfort the boy.

"We don't know," Carissa said softly, putting an arm around his shoulder.

Sammy began to cry. "But… she can't die!" he sobbed. "Don't let her die!"

"They're doing their best," Dustin said, trying to grab his hand.

"Lainey!" Sammy called, pulling away. He raced over to her as the paramedics placed her on a stretcher. "Lainey, can you hear me? Lainey!"

"Son, you've got to back away," said one of the officers.

"They found Tara! She's alive, Lainey! Did you hear that? You have to wake up so you can see her!" Sammy sobbed as the man pulled him back. "Lainey… don't leave us!"

261

Chapter 58

Three days later

Carissa

CARISSA AND DUSTIN arrived at the St. Paul Children's
Hospital around ten a.m. As they headed down the corridor, she
was suddenly overwhelmed by all of the different forms of energy
shared by patients and family members. Sadness. Grief. Hope.
Relief. By the time they reached their destination, her mascara was
a mess and she felt emotionally exhausted.

"Are you okay?" a nurse asked, when they stepped into the
room.

Embarrassed, Carissa dabbed a tissue under her eyes. "Yes.
This place does it to me. I always say I'm grateful for my psychic
gifts, but they're also a curse. Especially here."

"I understand," replied the nurse with a sad smile. "It's hard
enough working here every day, knowing you can only do so much
for some of these children. But, I wouldn't trade my job for the
world."

"And they're lucky to have you. It takes a special kind of
person to work here," Carissa said. "You're a gift to these
children."

"Thank you," the nurse said, her own eyes tearing up now.

Smiling, Carissa stepped over to where Lainey was lying. "How are you, sweetie?"

Lainey smiled from the bed. "Okay. I get to go home today."

"That's great news," Carissa said, breaking into a smile. It seemed like a miracle that she'd suffered little more than a concussion and a sprained wrist. "So, no more headaches?"

"Nope," she replied.

A sudden knock at the door made them all turn around. It was Sammy and his mother, Eaden.

"Can we come in?" Eaden asked, smiling at everyone. She was a striking woman with dark hair and bright green eyes.

"Of course," Beth said. "We were just talking about how Lainey gets to come home today."

"That's wonderful," Eaden replied. "You must be thrilled, Lainey."

"I can't wait," Lainey replied.

Sammy, holding a stuffed puppy and bag of candy, stepped over to the bed. Smiling proudly, he held the items out to Lainey. "I picked this out for you down in the store."

She took the items from him and hugged the puppy up to her cheek. "Thank you. He's so cute."

"You're welcome," he replied. "How is your wrist?"

"It hurts but they gave me some medicine," Lainey replied.

He nodded. "Good."

Carissa's heart warmed watching them together. She sensed that Sammy and Lainey's friendship would continue to grow, and because of what they'd been through together, help each other heal in many ways.

"So, what time do you get to leave?" Carissa asked.

"As soon as the doctor checks Lainey over," Beth replied.

"Oh, good." Carissa glanced around the room. "Where's Tom?"

"He's in the cafeteria getting some food," she replied.

From what Carissa had learned, Beth and Tom were trying to work things out.

Slowly.

She knew Beth had broken off her engagement to Mike and suspected that it was for more than just his cheating or the fact that his brother had taken her child. Carissa sensed that she still loved Tom, and that this ordeal had brought them closer than ever.

"I was wondering if you had a minute," Beth said to Carissa.

"Of course," she replied.

"We'll be right back, sweetheart," Beth said to Lainey, kissing her on the forehead.

"Okay," she said, playing with her puppy.

"Dustin, would you like me to get you some coffee?" Carissa asked him.

"That sounds good. Thanks," he replied.

Beth looked at Eaden. "How about you?"

"Oh, I'm fine. Thank you, though," she replied.

"Coffee, Sammy?" Beth asked with a smile.

He made a face. "No way. That's disgusting."

Laughing, the two women stepped out of the room.

"So, Lainey is doing well?" Carissa asked as they walked down the hallway toward the cafeteria.

Beth nodded. "She's been having some nightmares, but after everything she's been through, it's understandable."

"Definitely. I'm sure once she meets with the child psychologist, that will help, too."

"I hope so," Beth said. She let out a ragged sigh. "I'm just so relieved you help us find her. We were so close to losing Lainey, and... I just want you to know how truly grateful we are for everything you've done."

"I'm glad I could help," Carissa said. "When we're successful like this, there's no greater joy for me."

"I can imagine. Have you ever… not been able to return a child home?"

She nodded. "I'm still learning how to use this gift, and unfortunately, I've interpreted messages incorrectly. Kind of like I did earlier, when I thought Mike was involved."

"Messages? As in from beyond the grave?" Beth asked, looking intrigued.

Carissa smiled. "Something like that."

"Oh, here comes Tom. I know he wants to talk to you," Beth said as he walked toward them holding a tray of food.

Tom approached them with a warm smile on his face. Before he opened up his mouth to speak, Carissa already had an idea of what he wanted to talk to her about.

"Carissa. Nice to see you again," he said, looking genuinely happy.

She smiled. "At least this time it's a social call."

"Yeah, well," he sighed. "Speaking of which, I have something for you."

"You do?" Carissa replied.

He handed Beth the food tray and then reached into his jacket pocket. He pulled out a thank-you card with a splash of flowers on the front, and handed it to her. Inside was a personal note from Tom.

I wasn't just a jerk.

I was an idiot. And I was wrong.

Thanks for putting up with my ignorance and skepticism. But even more so, thanks for saving our little girl's life. We're forever in your debt. I know we'll never be able to thank you enough.

Sincerely,

Tom Brown

Smiling, Carissa looked at him. "I'm glad I could help. And from what it sounds like, you might have both your girls back in your life."

He grinned and put his arm around Beth. "You know, in a way, that was *also* your doing."

"No. That was all you," said Carissa. "Something tells me you two would have gotten back together despite my 'revelations' about Mike."

"I would like to think so," he replied.

Beth smiled. "All I know is that I'm happier than I've been in a while, despite everything that has happened."

"I can tell," Carissa said, feeling the warm vibes emanating off her.

266

"Oh, by the way, we're having a small 'Welcome Home' party for Lainey. In fact, Tara and her mother are going to be there. Sammy, too. We'd love it if you and Dustin could also join us," said Tom.

"That sounds wonderful. I bet Lainey and Sammy are going to be ecstatic to see Tara," Carissa said.

"Yes. She was released from the hospital yesterday and the kids weren't able to visit her. They were really disappointed," Beth said. "So I can't wait to see their faces when they see her today."

"You've been to see her, I heard. How is she doing, do you know?" Tom asked.

"Well, she definitely has a long road ahead of her," Carissa said sadly. "Medically, her leg will recover, the doctor said. Mitch's bullet only grazed her outer thigh. Had it been in an artery, she wouldn't be here right now."

"Wow," said Tom, shaking his head.

"Yeah, they don't think he intended to kill Tara," Carissa said.

"That's surprising," Beth said dryly.

"I know, right?" Carissa said, thinking about Mitch. He would have shot *her* without thinking twice. Something told Carissa that he didn't have the heart to kill the teenager, however. "Anyway, the poor girl went through hell, especially when she was first taken."

"They had her since she was eleven, right?" Beth asked.

"Yes." Carissa also knew Tara had been sexually molested and exploited, but didn't divulge that information. It wasn't her right.

"That poor child," Beth said, staring off into space. "I can't imagine what it was like for her or what those creeps did."

Carissa nodded. "More than we'll ever know, I'm sure. She is definitely going to need a lot of support and counseling. But you know, through all of the madness, she found the will to defy her abductors and help Lainey and Sammy. I think knowing that is going to help her heal, more than anything."

"Let's hope so. We owe her, that's for sure," Beth said.

"And Lainey can't say enough good things about her. Fortunately, it sounds like she was able to get them out of there before they were," a disgusted look spread across Tom's face, "assaulted."

"She did," Carissa said, knowing what he was really trying to say. Neither child appeared to have been sexually molested.

"Did they ever catch the guys in the Tahoe?" Beth asked. "The ones who almost killed you at Mitch's?"

"Unfortunately, no. But, Detective Samuels is trying to find out all he can about Anna Dubov. What we've learned so far is that she was originally from Grozny, but moved to America when she was sixteen."

"Really?" said Beth, frowning. "Was she involved with trafficking even back then?"

"Maybe. They don't know for sure, but... I feel like she was groomed from an early age to help the people who sent her here. A victim, too, in her own right."

"Crazy," Tom said as they stopped at the coffee machine.

"Child trafficking isn't just a horrible, horrible crime. It's big business. There are over 1.5 million victims in the U.S. alone. And worldwide," Carissa sighed. "I read somewhere that it was over twenty-million. They say it's starting to surpass weapon sales."

Tom and Beth looked shocked.

"If you think about it, what's even scarier is that there are so many sick, twisted people out there who support this behavior," Tom said, looking gutted. "What's this world coming to?"

"It's a frightening place to live," agreed Carissa.

"I'm just... so grateful you saved our little girl," Beth said with tears in her eyes. "And you risked your life to do it."

Carissa put her hand on Beth's shoulder. "Lainey was worth it. So was Sammy. They all are."

268

Chapter 59

Carissa

AS THEY DROVE away from Lainey's party, later in the day, Carissa smiled to herself as she remembered the joyful expressions on Lainey's and Sammy's faces when they saw Tara. They looked at her as a true hero, even if she still didn't feel like one herself. She knew the teen had deep feelings of guilt for not helping some of the earlier children the group had kidnapped. Which was why Carissa had cornered her in the kitchen.

"You weren't meant to save them all," Carissa told her as they were hovering over appetizers.

Tara looked at her in surprise.

"We all have paths in life. And pitfalls. Some have it much worse than others; you can definitely attest to that."

She looked down at her hands but remained silent.

Carissa continued. "I understand the regret you have. Forgive yourself. You have to."

"There were so many others kids," Tara said, her eyes filling with tears. "And… I did nothing."

"You did try, though, didn't you?"

Her eyes widened.

"You tried escaping once and they hurt you, badly. Don't beat yourself up for being terrified that it would have happened again. Because, it would have."

"How do you know?"

Carissa smiled and handed her a napkin for the tears that were beginning to roll down Tara's face. "My intuition is pretty good."

"That's right," she said, breaking into a smile. "My mother told me about you."

"Did Carol also tell you how she never stopped searching for you?" Carissa asked, knowing it was something Tara needed to hear.

Tara dabbed at her face. "Kurt told me she didn't even try, but… I don't know. I guess I thought she was too busy trying to care for the twins."

"She was definitely busy, but your mother loves you fiercely. Just like she does your siblings. The woman never stopped searching for you and never gave up."

Tara smiled sadly. "That's what she told me, too."

"Good. Believe her. You can also believe that she'll be a smother-mother for a very long time," Carissa said with a smirk. "You won't be able to go to the bathroom without her making sure you made it there safely."

Tara laughed.

"Seriously, though, you're a strong, brave young woman and you have a long life ahead of you," Carissa said, feeling it in her heart. She also sensed that Tara was going to get into law enforcement or something similar. She even told her.

"I was thinking I wanted to become an online investigator or something," Tara said. "So I can bust monsters like Kurt from hurting other kids."

"You'll be very good at it," Carissa told her, staring into her eyes. "Just remember that you won't be able to save everyone, but the ones you do… will make it all worth it."

"My mom said you specialize in trying to find missing children," Tara said.

"I don't know if I 'specialize' in it. It's where my path has directed me so far. I would love to help anyone who needs it," she replied.

Sammy suddenly ran into the room holding an iPad. There was music playing from it.

270

"What are you watching?" Carissa asked as Sammy grabbed a handful of chips.

"It's this app that lets you lip-sync to music," he replied, showing it to her.

On the screen was a girl around twelve or thirteen lip-syncing a song by Taylor Swift.

"Who's she? A friend?" Carissa asked. The girl was pretty, with her light brown hair and large green eyes.

"Not a close one. She's really popular on here, though," he replied. "She has like fifty-thousand followers."

"Can I see that?" Carissa asked, her gut suddenly filling with dread.

"Sure," he said, handing her the iPad.

Carissa noticed that the girl, whose online name was Emma-maze, had hundreds of videos. She watched a couple more, and although the videos were fun and cute, something about them worried her.

"Are you okay?" Tara asked.

She looked up. "Yeah," she replied, smiling. "I just... I don't know. All this online stuff the kids are into these days. It's a little overwhelming how much time they spend doing stuff like this. I mean, this girl has hundreds of videos, it looks like."

"That's why she's so popular," Sammy said, crunching on chips.

"Strangers can't look up any of her personal information, can they?" Carissa asked.

"Only if they ask her for it and she gives it to them," he replied.

As relieved as she'd been to hear that, Carissa still felt uneasy and didn't know if it had to do with the girl on the videos or something else.

"What are you thinking about?" Dustin asked as they headed to what he'd told her was a potential client's house.

She told him about the iPad.

"I've heard of that lip-syncing app. All the kids are crazy about it now. They can make and share music videos with their friends.

Even a lot of adults are into it." He frowned. "I'm sure it draws the freaks in, too."

"Yeah. That's what I was thinking," Carissa said, imagining it was yet another way for them to try and trap children. "I was watching Emma-maze, and… I don't know. I started getting that feeling of dread I get when something is about to go wrong."

"Do you think she's in danger?" he asked, frowning.

"I don't know," Carissa replied, wishing she had a better handle on her psychic abilities.

"Maybe we should contact her?"

"And say what? I'm a psychic and I think you might be in trouble?" Carissa said dryly. "I mean, who knows… I might be getting bad vibes about one of her followers."

"I see your point. You said she has thousands of them?"

"Yeah."

He let out a ragged sigh. "Maybe you should sign up for an account?"

"Maybe. Or, maybe I'll just go home and meditate to see if something comes to me?" she said, chewing on her lower lip.

"Home as in 'our' home?" he asked with a hopeful smile.

The last few days, Carissa and Dustin had been working on their relationship, and things were going well. They'd talked about moving in together, and she knew wedding bells were probably in their future. This was both good and bad. Good, because she loved the man with all her heart. Bad, because she wanted it to be a surprise when he finally asked, but she already knew he'd been shopping for rings.

"That depends on which house you mean," she said, smiling. "I told you before, I'm not moving into your place. It's cramped and we both need more space."

Especially if they were to have children, and Carissa wanted that.

272

"Yours isn't exactly a palace, either," he chided. "But, as long as we're on the subject…"

"Uh oh. What does that mean?" she asked, wondering suddenly if he was going to 'pop the question'.

"You'll see," he replied, biting back a smile.

"I wish you wouldn't have said that," Carissa said, turning on the music to try and block whatever the surprise was he had in store. A couple miles later, Dustin turned down a road that led to a newer development.

"Close your eyes," he said.

Carissa did as he asked, and when he stopped the truck, he told her to open them.

"What's this?" she asked, looking out the window at a snow-covered field that was close to a nature preserve and elementary school.

He grabbed her hand. "The location of our new home."

Her eyes widened. She looked outside again and imagined the two of them designing a house together. Moving in. Getting a dog. Starting a family.

"Obviously, we should make it official," he replied, reaching into his jacket pocket. He pulled out a small, black box. "I'm sure you knew this was coming."

Her eyes filled with tears as he opened it up, showing her the diamond engagement ring inside. "Maybe, I did. But… definitely not today," she said.

Dustin grinned. "Really? I actually surprised you for once?"

"For once? You're the one person who keeps me guessing," she joked.

"Good." He took the ring out. "What isn't a surprise to you, I hope, is how much I love you, Carissa."

"I love you, too," she said hoarsely.

"When we were apart, I was miserable. In fact," he looked at the ring, "I actually purchased this during that time."

"You did?" she asked, surprised.

"Yeah. I knew you were the only woman for me and that... no matter what it took, I was going to get you back."

Her heart felt like it was overflowing with happiness.

Staring into her eyes, he said, "So, what do you say? Will you do me the honor of becoming my wife?"

Too choked up to talk, she nodded.

He slid the ring on her finger and they kissed.

"Are you sure you didn't see this coming?" he asked, brushing away some of her fallen tears with his thumb.

"If I did I wouldn't have worn so much mascara," Carissa replied, laughing.

"You do look a little like a raccoon," he said with a tender smile. "But, you're my raccoon, and that's all that matters."

Carissa stared lovingly at him. Although she could tell that their future wouldn't always be easy, it would be filled with love and laughter. And, unfortunately... sadness. Sadness for the missing. The ones they'd work so hard to find but would somehow slip through their fingers.

Still, she knew that rough and bumpy path was theirs to walk together. No matter what heartache they'd endure along the way.

"So, should we get out and start plotting out the house?" Dustin said, nodding toward the property.

Excited at the idea, she nodded.

They got out of the truck, and for the first time in a long while, Carissa was able to focus on something joyful. Not only their new house, but their new life together as a married couple.

"So, how many bedrooms should we have?" he asked.

Knowing what he was really asking, she told him as many as he wanted.

"Are you saying you don't know how many children we're going to have?" he asked, his eyes widening.

Thankfully, she didn't. "Besides you?" she joked. "No."

Dustin laughed.

"I should probably call my mother," Carissa said, taking out her cell phone. "She's going to be so excited."

"Then she approves of me?"

"Of course! She loves you. Why do you think she makes so much strawberry rhubarb jam every year? She knows you're crazy about it. What is it she always says? Oh, yeah. 'The way to a man's heart is through his stomach'."

"And other body parts," he said with a wicked grin.

She rolled her eyes. "I'm definitely *not* sharing that fact with my mother."

He slid his arms around her waist. "Believe me, she might not be psychic, but she's a feisty Irish woman who was married to a cop. I'm thinking she already knows and probably has some secrets of her own."

Carissa smiled.

The end

Made in the USA
Columbia, SC
27 December 2017